Raule Dila'an De

Compiled By : **Neha.K.M , Parneet Kaur**

Spectrum Of Thoughts

AM/56, Basanti Colony, Rourkela, 769012, Odisha

An Affiliate Of FanatiXx

Website :- www.sotpublication.com

Published by Spectrum Of Thoughts 2022

ISBN : 978-93-5452-512-4
Typesetted By: Mayuri Valanju
Cover Designed By: Sagar Samal

ACKNOWLEDGEMENT

First and foremost, we would like to thank the Almighty for the reason we are here today.

We thank Every soul who helped us to bring this book a successful one.

We thank our head Mayuri Valanju and Divya Renwa for giving us an opportunity and also for their constant support till the completion of the project.

We thank Spectrum of Thoughts Publication team for providing this wonderful platform for me and the budding writers.

We thank all the co-authors of this anthology for being patient and keeping faith in us; co-operating, supporting and encouraging us in every step while making this Anthology.

We would like to give our heartily thanks to the Designer, Sagar Samal for giving such a wonderful cover page for this Anthology.

We also thank the Book Interior Designer, Mayuri for making the book a beautiful one.

DISCLAIMER

This Anthology is a melody of memories. The writers have beautifully described their every emotion through their write-ups and they have given their words that the write-ups are free from plagiarism.

So, if any plagiarism is detected in the book neither the publishing house nor the compiler will be responsible.

INDEX

Compiler : Neha K M

Compiler : Parneet Kaur

CO-AUTHORS

Theva Kiruba
Thelostinferno
Shongminthang Haokip
Dipshikha Sen Gupta
Saile Korukonda
Shravani Badhe
Umera Zafer
Harsha Ramachandran
Anushka Achrekar
Will Griffith
Sony Sehgal
Manpreet Singh
Harf Inder
Satkardeep Singh
Karanpreet Singh Khanna
Navjot Singh
Gurjeet Kumar
Ashna Kaur

NEHA K M
(Compiler)

NEHA K M was born and raised in the beautiful state Kerala ,Gods own country. A free soul and a wanderlust who, intimes, is a doodler. She has published her works in several anthologies and is now working as a Head Compiler at Spectrum of Thoughts Publication. As a compiler she has compiled an amazing anthology "ESTO TAMBIEN PASARA", which is sure to win your hearts, many more coming your way.

Instagram : i_dream_.of_unicorns_
Email id : neha.sot@gmail.com

The Solace Soul

Staring at the plain wall,

millions of thoughts passed as a movie screen!

The colourpencils depicts her ideas,

Her past sticks harder than the glue!

Worried, tensed, confused?

No, no, I am not!

I am blank!

My paints turned white, vanished !

I couldn't see my portraits,

Oh heart, don't be so hard!

I wish to paint!

I love to write!

I meet to think!

Please be nice to me!

Oh my heart!

Morning glimpse, my happy colours,

My paintings are still the same,

Brushes dried, not ever again!

Oh my love, its been days,

Where have you been?

Paint and canvas whispered!

She's back with her broken heart, brush replied!

Happiness aside!

Wondering those days moved like a waterfall,

No, she couldn't,

That was worse!

I have lost something,

My cozy corner felt lonely!

Dark nights she loved,those dim lights,

Her love for colours!

Still down, need a change?

She slept, doing nothing,

The cozy table aside!

Let she wakeup with happiness!

-Neha K M

PARNEET KAUR

(Compiler)

Parneet Kaur is a 19-year old, pursuing Btech and a shaeirah (poetess) who is writing heartily to express herself and her feelings through her words to the world.

IG: @the_shaeirahh

ਰੌਲੇ ਦਿਲਾਂ ਦੇ-

ਕੁੱਝ ਭਾਰੀ ਤੇ ਕੁਝ ਹੌਲੇ ਨੇ
ਇਹ ਸਭ ਦਿਲਾਂ ਦੇ ਰੌਲੇ ਨੇ
ਕੁੱਝ ਜ਼ਿਆਦਾ, ਤੇ ਕੁਝ ਥੋੜੇ ਜਿਹੇ
ਮੈਂ ਸਾਰਿਆਂ ਦੇ ਪੱਖ ਗੌਲੇ ਨੇ

ਮੂੰਹ ਮਿੱਠੇ ਦਿਲ ਤੋਂ ਕੌੜੇ ਨੇ
ਜਜ਼ਬਾਤ ਇਹਨਾਂ ਵਿੱਚ ਥੋੜੇ ਨੇ
ਮੈਂ ਜਿਹੜੇ ਰਾਹੀਂ ਤੁਰ ਜਾਵਾਂ
ਮਿਲਣੇ ਹੀ ਪਹਿਲਾਂ ਰੋੜੇ ਨੇ

ਗੱਲਾਂ ਤੋਂ ਲਗਦੇ ਭੋਲੇ ਨੇ
ਇਹ ਸਭ ਹੀ ਰਾਹੋਂ ਡੋਲੇ ਨੇ
ਕੁਝ ਹੁੰਦਾ ਮਾੜਾ ਵੇਖ ਕੇ ਵੀ
ਸਭ ਕੰਨੀਂ ਬਣਦੇ ਬੋਲੇ ਨੇ

ਸੌਖੇ ਜੋ ਰਿਸ਼ਤੇ ਖੋਣੇ ਨੇ
ਲਗਦੇ, ਔਖੇ ਨਿਭਾਉਣੇ ਨੇ
ਇੱਕ ਪਿਆਰ ਹੀ ਤਾਂ ਬੱਸ ਸਾਂਝਾ ਏ
ਬਾਕੀ ਸਭ ਜਿੰਦ ਦੇ ਰੋਣੇ ਨੇ

-Parneet Kaur

जिंदगी मेरे घर आना:

अश्कों को पनाह दे
आंखें तुम भर लाना
कह रहा दिल ये, कि
जिंदगी, मेरे घर आना

हां, उलझन बहुत है
सुलझाने तू चल आना
खुशियों की महफ़िल में
बनकर तुम ग़ज़ल आना

लगती है आदत गर
बुरी भी, तो बन जाना
रोकू मैं जब भी, तुम
एक पल तो थम जाना

दिल विल मिलाने की
बातें भी कर जाना
चाहता है दिल यूं, कि
जिंदगी, मेरे घर आना

-Parneet Kaur

Theva Kiruba

Theva Kiruba is an aspiring writer in her early twenties. She holds bachelor's degree in English and pursuing her Master's in Holy Cross College.

She is really enthusiastic about spending her time in writing. She has developed strong sense of writing poetry. She has published almost 50 poems , as well as a book titled "A Quill with Nectar Drop."

Authentic Claimer

On the whole, this humankind utterly roofed with extroverts. Frequently, we people assume that extrovert barely know how to outshine over introvert. These extroverts are able to socialize with the groups undoubtedly and accomplish the goals gallantly. Meanwhile, introverts are timid as well as tacit. Truly, I'm saying that, rather than extrovert, introvert accomplish heaps. Not barely in the civilization even in their delicate life.

On occasion people will act toward them as they are insignificant and not able to do a work with full buoyancy, bashful, hushed and unable to face plus socialize with the society. In actual fact that's not a faux pas, they are in the possession of autonomous world and existing in their own breathing space. Frequently, we are seeing one side of the introvert people, not other side of them. Introvert may be sluggish in decision making. But once they finalized with their decision, their preference are typically virtuous when we comparing them with extrovert traits. A good number of the legends admit themselves as an introvert. If a person is tacit or else combating with this world means, they are stronger than extrovert.

Introvert are enjoying their own company and exploring their inner self. They are really independent to imagine productively. They are breathing in their own breathing space. Introverts are stronger, even if they are unaided in their life. We have to give respect to their breathing space zone.

"**Being unaccompanied is not a blunder; really it's a enormous forte**,"

Destination in their own palm rather than where they from"

Internal appearance is always different from external one."

-Theva Kiruba

Solitary Tastes

A number of books are comprehended by fifty;
A few books are choosing by twenty;
De facto they utterly commensurate,
However they are unimaginable in their own way;
Culling be mere,
Whereas other side of coin is contrasting;
Integrity abide divergent,
Eccentricity prevail not either with aforementioned ardor;
Ardor may be more,
Ought not to chew at erstwhile;
Howbeit actually,
We pining, up to our mortal coil;
Arbitration's easy,
Notwithstanding breathing is a zephyr;
Yup!
They are quintessential!
We are peerless!
Everyone is archetypal.

-Theva Kiruba

True Blue

Exquisitenesses perhaps stumble;
Fallibilities are not their persistent mark;
Sporadically undeclared;
Erratically being throb;
Still and anon fondle timid;
Infrequently abide unescorted;
Seldom being feeble;
It mayhap steering,
Not until their existence;
Ratification is as scarce as hen's teeth;
Effectuating is provoked;
Frequently fall head over heels,
Yup! They are in "True blue".
Authentic shades of the cosmos!

-Theva Kiruba

Floret With Divergent Hue

They are not a dejected epilogue,
They are exceptional in contrast to others;
Their poles apart from an implicate,
They are fatalities;
They are not being on one's jack,
They are the master's of their sailing;
They are not a blunder,
They are in the precise relish;
They are not captives,
They unduly have ad lib;
They are not obelisk,
They too have tenderness;
They aspire to glide;
They have to mount,
With like chalk and cheese tincture.

-Theva Kiruba

Musing

I'm in the mid-dusk,
Standing in the balcony;
With half sipped coffee cup;
Tremendous blocks are four;
Gradually grows more and more;
Stepping out is not easy;
But, I'm trying hard,
So as crazy;
I'm the one who standing in the balcony standing all alone;
So threatening to open up myself;
My inner voice murmurs something;
You are worthy!
You are born to shine!
That's why I'm standing alone here;
Not sad but to shine...

-Theva Kiruba

Knitted Voice

She is drowning slowly;
Wonder why it's happening?
She knitted her broken pieces;
Lose one's head over is kid's stuff;
Habitually she is falling;
And persistently it's hurting her;
She skeptic her,
Why?
Her heart wants its kindred soul;
So she does;
In the halfway,
She standing alone with scares;
Assuredly, she gets through one's head,
She is the outshine ally for her;
Nobody can hit the bull's-eye to her,
Rather than her soul!

-Theva Kiruba

Husky Verso

Millennial recto swivel bygone;
Still, I feel my heart ache,
In that Choate phase;
No maneuver, No alleviation;
That drags me in,
Even if I try;
It nudges me to the chest,
Yup!
Chest of four barricades;
It's so suffocating;
Aloofly I staying underneath of the pages;
Pages are capsize,
With my meat hook;
When I reached,
Into the depth;
The deep long interior,
To the transparent of my heart;
I realize who I'm.

-Theva Kiruba

Magical Mystery

I unbolt my heart for her;
She is spare praiseworthy,
Than whatsoever thing in this cosmos;
My special soul mate!
Always I'm in my own world,
She is fine with real world;
Our interrelatedness is so profound,
Sometime I adored her rhapsodize;
All our giggling sound,
Echoing everywhere;
We both are loved to laugh and loved to fight;
Always my thought is to make her happy;
We allocate each other,
What we sequestrate;
More than get one's hands on;
It's a Magical Mystery!

-Theva Kiruba

Quarter Space

She needs downtime,
After big events;
Coz, she feels weird;
Half day in shopping mall;
Half quarter in workstation;
Finally she drained;
She craves into deep diving,
To the bowl of emotions;
Sometime feel like starving;
Sometimes feel low;
Her thoughts are linger in one box;
The recharge box!
She needs some space from their society;
That's all her;
Her own Universe!

-Theva Kiruba

Letter To My Mind

I need some time to think;
I need my own space to carve myself;
I'm not able to reflect,
Even, if I'm stressed;
These socializing people are big dosage;
My purpose is also to live and enjoy;
I feel low,
No energy in this compressed room of people;
I'm best at, what I'm;
Only need is space;
I'm valued people,
But I want to be in my own Universe;
Always I respect,
Who returns same thing to me;
I need space,
At least give me some space in your memory.

-Theva Kiruba

Thelostinferno

As an amateur, creative writer with a penchant for composing poetries and stories at the intersection of imagination and reality, thelostinferno depicts the profound aspects of life in a way thta is spiritually uplifting to many. Thelostinferno aims to establish herself as a prolific writer for people across geographic and societal boundaries and has already published a select few compositions in two anthologies.

Melanin

How magnificent is the canvas,
That HE designed for his creation,
HE set the most beautiful tones,
As an embodiment of his imagination.
Like a picturesque harmony,
HE painted HIS muse,
But never forget HE chose black,
To highlight HIS chosen hues.

With brush strokes of perfection,
And drops of pigment,
HE finished HIS masterpiece,
That enlivened HIS figment.
And then as a potter,
HE took some clay,
And molded the characters,
Of HIS divine play.

Known for HIS benevolence & compassion,
HE ensured equality,
HE added a myriad colors to his sculpture,
Only one color? How could it be?
The cosmos came to life,
And so did man,
Behold! his creation is colorful,
Brights, pastels, or tan.

HIS crafts also have imperfections,
They all have flaws,
Don't preach flawless beauty,
It defeats HIS grand cause.
Don't let the world fool you,
Don't let insecurities creep,
Your skin color is only MELANIN,
Real beauty is skin deep.

Different is your skin tone,
But RED is your blood,
Strengthen your humanity,
Don't let tears of oppression flood.
HE doesn't have a skin tone, HE loves us all,
Stop the venom of racism from spreading today,
Before it paralyzes and makes mankind fall.

-Thelostinferno

The Hummingbird

Flapping the wings of creativity,
With fleeting visits to vivid thoughts,
The hummingbird makes her presence known,
With her vivacious imprints in many spots.

Boisterous is her nature,
But "recluse" is her preferred name,
Her curious mind fits profound memories,
Like a universe squeezed in a tiny frame.

Defying the definition of ordinary,
With others she doesn't sway,
Mystical and confounding are her traits,
You can't comprehend her in just one way.

A vibrant misfit amidst many of her league,
She hovers around in her own sky,
Admire her till she flitters around you,
Because one day, her soul will fly.

-Thelostinferno

The Flight

She stood aloof, staring at a myriad known, yet somehow unknown faces across the room.
She looked at everyone, but could not feel or express her feelings anymore.

Some detachments had numbed her.
Some struggles had left her emotionally paralyzed.
Her stay was welcomed by many, yet she knew it was a temporary welcome.

But this time, it hit her different.
She was oblivious to all around her. Nobody could see her true self anymore. All the things they knew about her left her perishable, mortal body.

She now stood by the window alone. A cool breeze ran threw her hair and touched her pale white skin.
She immersed herself with the cold, whistling sound of the air.

The coolness of the air dried the blood and sweat around her shackles.
She felt lighter.

A peace that she had never felt in centuries.
Shackles of burden finally began to twist and open. She slowly levitated in the cold air.
And in a lightning speed, she took the final flight.

-Thelostinferno

The Walking Lens

Mumbai. An overcrowded city bustling with eyes full of dreams. A city that is known to enchant many with its indomitable spirit. A city that comes alive at night. A city that is a refuge for theunsheltered and the opulent.A destination for many individuals who wish to capture its enigma and love to immerse themselves in its mesmerizing beauty.

One such wanderlust-hungry individual is Ahmed- a young, 20-year-old photographer, residing in a chawl in Dharavi, who wishes to become the best travel photographer in India. An ambivert by nature, Ahmed was known to be a silent observer, a young man who would not engage in social interactions like others,but whoexpressed his thoughts incessantly through his blogs covering various undiscovered nooks and corners of the city. "The Walking Lens" is what his friends and acquaintances prefer to call him, as he considers his eyes to be the best camera in the world. Ahmed weaves stories wherever he goes; with a good-quality camera-containing phone and with his innovative ideas, Ahmed portrays Mumbai in a way seldom portrayed by anyone. From a puddle of water reflecting the charisma of sunrise and sunset, to the silhouettes of people jogging on the beach in the wee hours of morning against a backdrop of vivid hues, Ahmed depicts the liveliness of the city with cleverly drafted quotes and captions known to garner admiration from people for his art and the city.

On one such photography assignment, Ahmed encountered the most memorable night of his life. It was a moderately bustling, cold night. Ahmed was on his way to his humble abode, when suddenly he stumbled upon a wounded street dog. Street dogs are a common resident of Mumbai streets, a formidable force against robbers or anti-social elements prowling at night. As Ahmed began examining the dog, he was heartbroken to find that someone had deliberately hit the dog for barking at night. As a true animal lover, Ahmed contacted a few friends who worked at animal NGOs.

Fortunately, he could establish contact with an NGO hospital operating at odd hours of the night. However, it was distant and he did not have a vehicle to reach the destination. He was searching for one when suddenly, an unfamiliar voice called out to him.

"Excuse me. Do you have a problem? Do you need my help?". A coarse feminine voice interrogated him. Ahmed found the individual to be a trans woman, a sex worker. The COVID pandemic had hit many businesses and many people lost their livelihood. The pandemic also affected the income of sex workers as people avoided visiting them to prevent contraction of the disease. Ahmed was reputed to be an empath, a person who responded to other people with compassion and attempted to understand their plight. So, being questioned by such a person did not affect him at all. "Yes yes, please! I really need to get this injured dog to an NGO hospital. It's badly hurt." As soon as he responded in the affirmative, the sex worker took her scooty, a humble Indian vehicle given by her friend, and told Ahmed to sit behind her and carry the dog in his arms. Traffic at such an odd hour of the night is unusual in Mumbai, but that day, the traffic was frustrating. Nonetheless, both decided to help the dog come what may. Within an hour of the journey, they reached the NGO hospital building and the dog was operated upon. They were advised to keep the dog under observation at the hospital. Breathing a sigh of relief, they both decided to drink some tea at a nearby tea stall.

After all, they both realized that it was daybreak and the entire night drifted away in treating an injured dog. While conversing with the sex worker, Ahmed realized what a troublesome, wretched, and risky life they lead. She spoke at length about how the pandemic hit her life and income and how she would love to enroll in a vocational course to improve her life and future, but finances were a hurdle to her dreams. Ahmed listened to her patiently and then contacted a friend who dealt with the rehabilitation of women and who could help her enroll in courses that could usher a positive development with limited finance.

Days passed. The dog recovered and became stable. The sex worker had enrolled in a professional data entry course and was offered a humble position in a good organization. She thanked Ahmed for his guidance and help. Ahmed continued with his photography assignments as usual and thanked the One in Heaven for making him a wallflower, a silent observer if you may say.

Owing to his observation, he could help a mute injured animal and an individual in dire need of money and stability.

Conclusion: Being a wallflower maybring about opportunities to help others. One needs to be observant and helpful. There are perks of being a wallflower.

-Thelostinferno

Shongminthang Haokip

Shongminthang Haokip is an Indian overseas working professional by day, thinker and a dreamer by night. He studied English (hons degree) at Modern College, Imphal and then MBA from Amity University, UP. With a sense of poetry at heart, he deeply cares about people struggling with love, spirituality and humanity. Find more of his works and updates at www.shongwrites.com or can be reach out at gghaokip@gmail.com

Soulmate Is A Gift

A gift as expensive as priceless
Invaluable is its worth and
Incomparable is its value
More than we owned
We treasured them
Even when you don't see still
you can feel
If children's are God's gifts
what would be your gifts as a single
other than your soulmate who will
consider you as God's gift
While others owned you
Your soulmate will
treasure you.

-Shongminthang Haokip

My Dream For A Future Manipur

My dream and only hope for my people
born and unborn

That one day in Manipur the new sunrise
equally shines on all people
Without any shadowed of opportunity
across the hills as in the valley

To the peaceful coexistence where
all people feel home safe and secure

To the days when our freedom fighters are
honored as National heroes
To the sanity where we see one another
as neighbors; not as foreigners

To the days where people are helping instead of hurting
And filled all hearts with humility and humanity
as one Manipur.

-Shongminthang Haokip

Beyond My Imaginary World

In our planet earth
True destiny I find no place
Instead only priorities keep changing
In my younger years it was ambitions
That success is but achievements alone
As I grow older I find purpose
The meanings of life
Memories in itself ingrained
The connections
The trust
The love
Beyond my imaginary world
There's bountiful purpose driven life
Wonderful creation in itself
Reasons to live and learn.

-Shongminthang Haokip

Impatience In Spirituality

For a man faithful to his faith
And righteous to it's divine path
There's no fear but
dreams and hope
Humbled me dare not question God's plan
After having seen all unfailing promises
It's only my human impatience being
Oftentimes wonder—
The Wait...!
How long? O Lord!
When?
Without questioning
Silently my sobbing soul seeks
An Almighty Answers.

-Shongminthang Haokip

Mysterious Dreams

Every time I wake up with dreams
my consciousness stretches beyond
this body and mind
Yes, I live in two-dimensional paradigm
From a spiritual realm to this mortal world
Though mysterious than a mycelial network
My soul guides me through in tranquil
Instill hopes from fear and cognizance
From human's dementia
Of confused mind full of anxiety
Science may called it data dump
Or useless memories as such
Scientists still seeks to interpret
Infinite symbols of dreams
As they invoke feelings perplexed
Though when my ethereal soul shepherded along
I find clarity in my mysterious dreams.

-Shongminthang Haokip

Fearless Mind

Fear not your fear
It's a mindset that intimidates
Think harder but take it easy
Speak freely with fewer words
Soft but sharp in meanings
Utter the right language
In the right manner
Be kind but firm
Strong but never be rude
You're a born change maker
It's only but a self-realization
Of who you are!
Take a deep breath
Listen to your soul
And embrace your fearless mind.

-Shongminthang Haokip

Mystic Glance Of Your Eyes

That looks I see
from your loving eyes
killing me alive
a thousand times!
Can't figure out even
why am I so obsessed?
Beyond distance and distraction
even behind glasses blocking apart,
Your loving eyes traverse like flashlights;
nor sounds neither lights can't surpassed.
This chemistry of your glance
even laws of physics can't fathom;
but only my poetic feelings can.

-Shongminthang Haokip

This World

Though part of my poetic soul finds
Serenity in every essence of life
from the fresh air I breathe
to the paradisal natures around
or the affections I have for humans
and the fulfilling lives of other species.
And yet despite every reasons to rejoice
part of me feels I don't belong here
where human minds are corrupted with
perceptions filled with selfishness
driven by emotions and destructive ego
I find no place to take my soul at peace
only but lesser people to trust
as I long for eternal bliss.

-Shongminthang Haokip

Dipshikha Sen Gupta

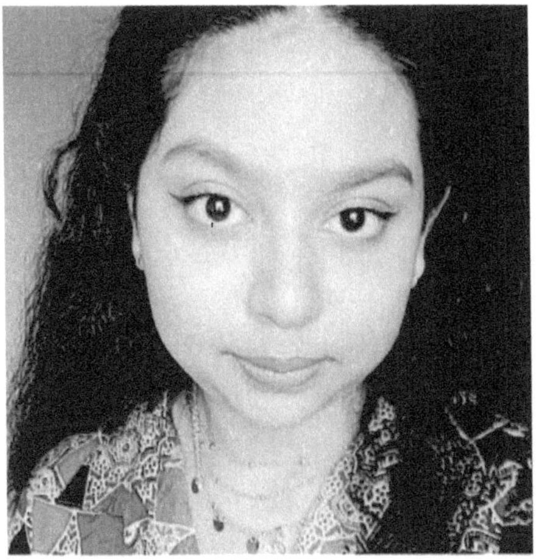

Dipshikha Sen Gupta, grew up in Kolkata, India. She is a seventeen-year old High school student who wishes to become a literature student in future. She likes to create art and write to express her artistic self. She, earlier this year, had taken part in an anthology as well. She likes to read and listen to music. Her inspirations are mostly her surroundings and her experiences. She has been an introvert all through her life and felt as an outsider in this world. In this piece of writing she wanted to express herself and let others know that no matter how quiet introverts are they have the loudest voice and needs to be heard by everyone. You can find her @_dipshikhasengupta on instagram and email at dipshikhasengupta03@gmail.com

IT IS OKAY TO BE AN INTROVERT.

I'm not shy, I'm not weird, I'm anything but social and that's fine with me. No, I don't find it boring to be in my own room in my own comfort doing things that inspires me to be better self and doing things that helps me to grow as a person. You might either find it completely nonsensical or completely relatable.

All my little life that I've lived till now I've been a person who doesn't like to be around too many people, and I don't think that is weird at all and I often hear people asking me to socialize as if they are helping me, though I don't blame them because they never know what I like. I'm an introvert and it is not like I'm shy or I want to avoid people or I hate them, I just am more comfortable as an unnoticed individual among a big field of people, does that mean I don't know how to speak up or to stand up for myself ? No, I know exactly how to do these but I don't like unnecessary attention as well as I find it hard to talk amidst a large crowd.

Growing up in a joint family as well as having around too many celebrations in the family all around the year I would say I was often forced to enjoy those moments of socialization and I had to follow up as I didn't know any better. But at the end of your adolescence while you are almost done with the first half of your education and you almost have become an adult and you are strictly asked to choose with what you want to do with the rest of your life, I guess you deserve the power of deciding on behalf of yourself that what do you want to prioritize- YOUR COMFORT OR YOUR VANITY.

I had to face many situations where I've been demeaned for being an antisocial, for being a homebody, even by my close surroundings. In my school as well I don't have too many friends, well frankly speaking to you I only had a couple who I considered to be my friends and even though nobody said this to me but sometimes I criticize myself wondering about my vanity that others might think that I don't socialize because I'm arrogant or rude. I don't talk much because I've zero self confidence when it comes to 'breaking the ice'. I'm just too afraid of being judged or being taken for something which I'm not. Thinking about all this often makes me uncomfortable and anxious. Even though I might know the correct answer but I feel too under confident and flustered to raise my hand. It feels like everyone is looking at me and paying attention to me, making my nerves shake. All through my early school life the only remark I got from my teacher on my report card was that I'm a very quite child and I don't interact much . All those social family function which I requested to my parents, if I could skip but have been forced to attend unwillingly. Also all those time when I've been nagged for hours to go to a place where I know no one. Those times were nightmares to me. Does nobody understand how hard it is for me to cope with all this? Does nobody care? I still don't know.

Here's how I see it, as I said I don't necessarily hate people but I just don't want to deal with them, I just don't want to take part in the unhealthy play of 'what's going on in your life and let me judge you on the basis of that and help you to increase your anxiety'. I don't want others to know about my life, I just simply don't want other's opinion to guide my life and break my privacy. When I go to any social event, I feel lost, I feel too overwhelmed and then too tired after greeting people, and I feel instead of taking part in this social meetings and getting yourself drained off of your energy I'd better use that energy to focus and create something meaningful. And if you are reading this book then perhaps you too are alike me and would understand my point of view. All this while you've been reading about how it sucks to be an introvert in a world full of extroverts but here's the part for appreciating our existence in this world. The perks of being an introvert, I enjoy myself the most when I'm alone, I feel so much relaxed, so much me. I breathe comfortable in my skin. I don't care about the world and it's deeds. I find myself through my belongings in my space and not in other people's eyes. I get inspired, I create and I bring out feelings and pour it into the world. I genuinely love to be just by myself. I, an introvert have a quiet approach to life. Even though my mouth is shut for hours but my mind is processing and thinking ideas continuously. I have small group of friends but I form deeper connection with them, I value quality more than quantity. Small talks are a big no for me, I'm incapable of starting a conversation, but if you start speaking I'll be the most patient listener you've come across. I do enjoy good company as well. I appreciate deep conversations but not forced greetings.

People who are loud are taken to be confident and filled with ideas by the world but perhaps may be the quiet introvert sitting amongst is easily forgotten or not seen to be capable of having ideas just because she is not loud like others. In this world filled with people who have a lot to say and no one to listen, it lacks peaceful times. The world has always doubted the introvert's capability to be strong and powerful. In schools from an early age we were taught to be vocal, to raise hands and participate in discussions. After growing up we are expected to be social and outgoing to be liked by others. Don't misunderstand me, I don't discourage these ideas but I would like to know that as much as we want to improvise people all through their life span, instead can't we just accept people as they are? An introvert is a quite individual but that doesn't mean they are not interested or their head is empty. You could possibly get the best ideas from an introvert, because they take time to think about their ideas more than giving out they like to take in from a conversation. The quiet strength of an introvert can perhaps shake the world.

So at the end who are introverts? Well, introverts are individuals who have a quiet approach to their life and they take time to process, think and observe their environment. They like to surround themselves with less number of people who they value and who values them. Introverts might not be loud but that doesn't mean that they are depressed or unhappy. They too are pretty cool, they too can have fun but just let them recharge themselves after long hours of socialization. For relaxation the introverts don't require to hang out with big group of friends, they find pleasure in things where the mind is focused and concentrated. In this huge world of demanding extroverts if you, an introvert, find it difficult to sustain know that introverts are everywhere just like you and me they too want to escape the loud noises of the urban city. Find your peace, maybe read a book or listen to music and create a bubble that gives you comfort.

I am an introvert and I find myself to be very interesting and the deep conversation that I've with myself are so valuable to me that I can't afford to lose it just for the sake of making new friends. I like to give my time and my mind the space to my thoughts. I'm okay being an introvert. Oh, and did I mention that I'm not lonely at all rather I enjoy my own company very much.

-Dipshikha Sen Gupta

Saile Korukonda

The author is a resident of the city of pearls, India. She is an Assistant Professor by profession and writing is her passion. She is interested to write poems, short stories and quotes. Writing has been her passion since childhood and she continued it along with her professional life.The author says that writing boosts up her mind and also help to be the biggest refreshment for the packed professional lifestyle.Ig:@ones.heartfelt.thoughts

WALLFLOWER

You call me a wall flower,
Never mind u never knew what do I shower.
I may not mingle with many,
And that's where I don't hurt any.
I need no gossip,
I'm always comfortable with my own coffee sip.
I'm not lost in my dreams,
Rather a deep thinker which is a treat.
I am a great listener; you don't find many
I am a vigilant observer, you can't see in any
I don't boast upon myself, 'coz publicity is not my nest
I am clear at my vision,
I don't rely on anyone's decision.
I enjoy my own company
Just gazing at people's strategy.
I am the one whom u can trust blindly
As I don't socialize and break your confidentiality.
A wallflower is as beautiful and cheerful
Just like a lotus in pond.
People say that a wall flower is a lonely person
But I say a wallflower is person with inner solitude who is at exuberance.

-Saile Korukonda

A Hobby

A Hobby makes you think
And let's others wink.
It refreshes your mind and thoughts
Be it the smallest of all or the biggest of all
Do anything that makes u joyful
Hobbies are a great stress buster in our all-day workaholic life.
My hobby is to write. Be it a single line quote or lines of poetry all the thoughts I pour down on the paper. It makes me feel relaxed and eases my mind
I feel that most of us as we grow older, tend to get involved into life's busy schedules. And forget the hidden talents of our childhood." Let's wake up the child in us and explore the new us". Spending hours in bringing out the best of it gives oneself much more pleasure and happiness.
A break into the thoughts of our hobbies could be our success mantra as well. Never leave your hobby.

-Saile Korukonda

Never Give Up

Its all about the way u think
Positivity lifts to the heights
Negativity make u shrink
Maintain peace of mind
And not make rubbish wind
You are no less to anyone
You are the only masterpiece one.
If the situation is tough
Show that you are the toughest
If they say you can't
Shut them with your success.
Be cheerful, laugh louder,
serve the needy, learn always
You may not win the marathon but
NEVER EVER GIVE UP

-Saile Korukonda

Shravani Badhe

Shravani Badhe is teenage writer/author from Pune, Maharashtra. She started writing since her school days and instantly fell in love with words. Her writings are basically a reflection of her thoughts. She loves poetry a little too much. She has already been a Co author of the anthology "The Act of Perseverance" with Spectrum of Thoughts . This was her first anthlogy to be part of and since then she's interested in them.

Mail Id : caffeineandpoetry@gmail.com

Anxiety At Fault

I always wondered
What to do
When they sang to me
Happy Birthday to you!

All the claps with the wishes
And also constant calls
Got me thinking
Why was I even born afterall

Extra attention was given
Wasn't very fond of it
Desired for some space
But couldn't even admit

Yes,I don't like interactions
Nor being social too
Call me an introvert
And just walk away from here ...shoo!

-Shravani Badhe

The Perk Of Distance

You call me to interact
Towards the social crew
Where each criticizes another
I wish they themselves knew

If I have to mingle
Only to get hate
Then I'm better off alone
With my drink along the plate

If you can't stand judgments
Being antisocial is a perk
It actually stops people
From meddling in your work

You can call me a wallflower
Who enjoys from a step
Letting the distance stay
I let people do the prep

-Shravani Badhe

Reasons Being Told

From the brightest days
To the darkest stay
In various phases I've grown
Went through them
With no hope of ray
And then I was left all alone

Looked for a fault,maybe mine
A mistake that was a sign
Of each one's mess,I solely own
But by me none were hurt
Still I took all the dirt
And then I was left all alone

All this affected quiet deeply
Started maintaining distance briefly
And then you ask me why don't I talk
Well I used to but now I don't
Wished you'd understand but you won't
I'm reserved now with each one blocked

My favorite task is to now avoid
Being social makes me annoyed
Call me a loner or even a wallflower
But that's now what I desire
Got a mirror to now admire
I'd address my personality as a superpower

-Shravani Badhe

The Effort To Avoid

Took a glimpse of this side
And turned to other
Got social anxiety already

A whole room with human interaction
Haunting me
Calling me to open up

Being aware of the scene
Avoiding successfully
Everyone and everything .

An approach was made
Took steps behind in hurry
Mission distancing was completed

Most motives were carried out
Of staying in the corner
Willingly and quietly

All that efforts of staying away
From each individual were made
Reason being an introvert
Shy and awkward....

She Who Stood In The Corner

When everyone was celebrating and partying, she was seen alone in a corner. She looked like moon among all those stars who refused to mix up and preferred shining alone... Many thoughts and opinions were instantly attracted in different minds just by looking at her

Some questioned her "Manners": Why is she like that standing away from everyone? Does she not have the manners to meet and greet? Some doubted her "Nature": What does that girl even get by just staying away like that? She must have a rude nature , she just seems stubborn. Some assumed the "Ego": What an egoistic girl! What harm did she even have in approaching us with a 'hey'! Her Ego will definitely backfire her ownself one day.

Well,she was a girl with manners and no one had the rights to question them just because she preferred some space for her ownself. No, she wasn't rude nor was she stubborn. It was her nature to stay away from them due to her own reasons and that does not make her behavior bad. Just because she didn't approach anyone and was by her ownself doesn't conclude her being egoistic. She was just unwilling to gather and didn't have intentions to potray any sort of Ego.

People like her exist. They are too nervous to gather around everyone and deal with social anxiety everyday. The reason can be their own insecurities, a quiet nature or maybe they are introverts. Such individuals are addressed as Wallflowers and potrayed with a negative image in the society. This needs to be changed. Introverts and wallflowers need to understood and respected too. It is for a reason they are like this and everyone is required to accept these facts. Stop judging them, pointing at them and start allowing them to have their own space which every wallflower desires to have.

-Shravani Badhe

Umera Zafer

Umera Zafer She is a writer by passion, expressing through words, Living the dream.

The Odd Girl

She was one of the shy Girls, Who never raised her hand even though she knew the answer
She always feared that she would be left out and tried to fit in
Little did she know that its the world who needs to blend in her ways and she has nothing to fear.
She was the odd girl and was always judged because what was normal to the world
was fascinating for her
For the world 2+2 is 4, but she wondered and questioned it to be 22 and not 4
Her way of thinking was different from others, she would find perfection even in the most un perfect situation, she would find comfort in discomfort, she found a way to turn her pain to pleasure and slowly but gradually she started to accept herself,
And was labelled as crazy and imperfect but she was crazy and imperfect for the world because the world tries to blend in, but not she because she was perfect in her own ways, comfortable in her skin, in love with her craziness and so she didn't care to be a wallflower in a world full of roses.
Because to her she was perfect even with her imperfections.

Its not always what you see.

She has the Prettiest Smile, but behind it she hides the deepest scars
She laughs in the daylight and with the rise of sun her smile tends to be brighter than the Sun
But when alone she cries a million tears
But her tears fall in front of his creator
Because she learnt it the hard way, that nobody belongs to you
And the world will Judge you even if you blend with it or stand out
Everyday as the sun rises she prepares herself for an unknown battle
and with every dawn she is a better person, a different person a strong person
Everyday she mends one broken piece
and with every piece that she mends she becomes unbreakable
soon she would be a fire filled with fear for the world
Soon she would be unbreakable
soon she would break the world being a wallflower

because being a wallflower is her greatest strength.

If you have the ability to Love
then love yourself first
because what you sow is what you reap
and self love is the best love

-Umera Zafer

Harsha Ramachandran

Harshavardhini Ramachandran love to read books especially the writings of Khalil Gibran. She says stories and poetry always give her elation. Pening down her thought is one of her leisure activities among crocheting and cooking. She has published in many anthologies including The days of our life, Treats and Treasure, Cuppa poetry, What are you gonna do about it? and The Treasure Island.

Being A Wallflower

Love thyself. Love is the best Jewel we give ourself. We should love ourselves in the way we are. How many of us love oneself without any regrets and disrespects? I sometimes think, is it wrong being an introvert? Maybe the extrovert will have the same question (Is it wrong being an extrovert?) Unless we love ourself in the way we are, our life is a misfortune and we feel like a misfit in this world.

I am shy, silent and I don't engage with people easily. It takes time for me to get close with someone, I'm comfortable only with a few. I think a lot before speaking to someone around me. I fear to mingle with strangers and the anxiety in me grows stronger when I see someone confident walking over me. It goes on, but I love the way I'm. I love myself for whatever reason it is or for every reason it is. I love the whole me, exactly as I am without any regrets.

'Wallflower' the name given for who doesn't mingle with people or whosoever doesn't engage socially. Do I always get anxieous when I'm around people? Why I prefer to be lonely all the time? There are often questions asked by people. Every person in this world is unique in their ways. One loves pop other loves classic; we can't go and blame their likes and dislikes. I am not afraid of people, of course I love to be with people and I'm not always a lonely flower. Every flower has its garden. I'm shy at times but I'm not fragile. I feel people around me are more confident and strong but not that I'm timid or pessimistic. I have belief in me that I'm strong enough to tackle any problem that comes my way.

I might not love to dance and sing in front of people. But I enjoy my own world. I dance, and my curves move to the beat of the music when I am surrounded with my close ones. One of my favorite thing to do is to dance with the music loud, in my room, without any eyes watching. That doesn't mean I'm anxious rather I prefer this way, just a choice of my living.

People ask, how do you feel when you are alone? I am not alone and I can't always be lonely and I have never been. I have my books and music to soothe me. And it is not that I don't speak with people. I have a close circle and my friends to laugh out my sorrows. I always have a shoulder besides me to cry and forget about the bitter things that happen in life.

It is that, we do sometimes need that solitude to enjoy our real self. To live in the moment that we wish to be in. I enjoy travelling and when I'm with nature, I become enthusiastic. I tend to have this ability in me, a natural habit, to observe people and the happenings around me.

Everyday starts in her lap. Nature. One thing I adore the most in this world is her. I always wonder how she grabs all my heart. She knows how to flatter me. Yes she does. I become a bystander, to perceive every inch of beauty she posses. I merge into her and have a feel of oneness. She is calm, silent and observing most of all, patient for all the things that we do her. Until, she reaches the wrath, with the destructions that arise to teach us a lesson. From the moment of waking up till the darkness encircles me, I love being with her.

I wake up with the sound of light,
Gleam passing the glass bright

That glitter upon my face;
The yellow son comes
Cracking the sky every morning

With the ray of hope in me,
I always rise without mourning.
Through the windows, I gaze
To seize the beautiful bliss
With the nature's morning kiss.

Tranquillity, me and her,
Moist breeze that nudge
Mist souse the vibration,

Soothes every ounce of my blood;
That shape my mood
And, prepare the day
With the esctastic vision I gay,
For the luminous creation
Incentive I grow,
With the espy I behold.

Hillock and green hues, I see

Groves spread over
Birds warble the tree
Here and there,
Playing with their partners;
Whirling around the garden

Butterflies throng fine blossoms
To entwine in the nectar;
Glory be to the creator
For this blithe spirit in my Eden.

Day and night
Like the people around,
Better know what is your choice.
I am always mute,

Try to live in solitude,
Neither a day I regret to bloom
Nor live my life in gloom.

My heart speaks and eyes listen
The World full of noise,
Quietness all around me!

Noticing everything around, being an observer is one different feel. As I said, I do enjoy watching nature, as a traveller I try to capture the best moments that I witness. Also I like to watch people, to watch all the nine emotions -

blithe, wrath, agony and more. I laugh seeing their happiness and weep seeing them cry. What all they do I love to watch how they cook, write, play, dance, fight, each and every action I ought to notice. Maybe the wallflowers are astute and sharp in grabbing things and actions that happen around them. They are sagacious, I think.

Starting from my school days till today going to the college, I use bus to travel. Bus rides though sometimes irritate are awesome experience in life. It is a feast for me to witness all sort of happenings and we are swarmed by different kinds of people. I become a silent observer and grasp everything that happens around me in the bus.

Bus rides are miscellaneous
Traffic and crowd bustles round
I turn taciturn and perceiving,
To glean the throbbing crowd around.
Street vendors here and there in the
stop,

Ready to hop;
Chips and Murukku,
Hot sundal and its pervading smell,
Sliced pineapples and raw mangoes
With the Sprinkling of chilli powder
Are tempting and delectable;
Sometimes irked, who hurl upon
And for horns blast in the ears
That rhymes with the clamour.

Always wanting the window seats,
Keenness to behold the happenings
Winter days and moist air
With the background of music
Vibrant and elevated,

That gladden the heart.
Love blossoms circling around

Speaking with eye language
And Smiles and whispers,

Throng the young couples.

Oldies pose the seats
With a face of innocence and authority

Where our humble gesture is a sacrifice.
Amongst the crowd, holding the pole,
Driver's sudden breaks mortify us

Straight we go and fall upon someone,
Someone behind will fall upon us
With an elaborate smile, Sorry!

Valorous and enthralling it is,
Buoyant memories I have some.

Laughters and chatters
Giggles and hummings
Sprightly with whistle sounds
Bus rides are a good shot!

When we be ourself we can definitely enjoy even the pain that comes our way. We will know how to handle and tackle the situation if we face them. Our own self is to be loved and cared enough to achieve more in our life. The belief in us is the prior thing needed in life to succeed whatever is wished for. The folk tongues will ridicule us, if we bother and stand with our heads down or worrying never helps us. We need to stand like a pole even in the stormydays.

We should develope our insight and self-esteem. If we stand and feel for what others think it will destroy our journey. The peace in our life will be ruined if we bother others opinion. Live the way you want it, do things that gives you happiness not others. Unless it is for the goodness of ourselves, our society and the people; the goals, we desire can be earned in any right ways. We definitely have innumerable ways to achieve what we desire for, when we listen to what our heart says. Sometimes the route that we choose may lead us to a wrong destination but we'll learn to lead a successful journey. We have many guardian angel around us, to help us and nurture us.

Am the queen of my world
Ready to whirl,

I love myself in the way I am
Why would I heed the bygone
Who never last long.
O listen! ardent souls

Ascertain what you deserve,

Mark the words of your heart,
May you hark the voice of thy soul;
To crave the best in you,
To withstand the obstacles,
To standby ur dreams,

Love yourself
In the way you're!
This is the time to think

Ought not to shrink
Thoughts to be built,
Not to live in guilt.
Find the zeal of life,

Respect what your heart yearns
Burgeon the path
And be the reason for your flame

Ready to burn the falter thoughts

-Harsha Ramachandran

Anushka Achrekar

Anushka Achrekar is a budding poetess who is passionate about capturing the thoughts about anything beautiful she comes across which coveys her messages to the society at large especially to the people she is connected with.

Thoughts Of A Wallflower

Sitting at a height all alone

Sipping the glass of Bourgogne wine

Being secretive is what i love to be

Watching the city lights and the sea

Giving myself a lot of time,

Exploring about myself is what i like

I observe the colors of the people as they pass by

Painting the rainbows in my way & how i like

that is what make's my heart stronger & stronger deep inside

-Anushka Achrekar

I Am Nobody

I am nobody,
They don't see me
But, you do

Don't worry they don't see us,

It's just me and you

I will show you the truth, I will show you the lies

Hurtful changes

As time passes by

Some remain warm as fire & some turn cold as ice

Our enemies were for good

& our few close ones of dirty secrets & lies

One day they are going to know,

I am somebody

But just for today,

Let me see the truth of the world

& be a Nobody

-Anushka Achrekar

A Silent Voice, With Massive Thoughts

A silent voice, with massive thoughts

over people i prefer talking to the walls

I talk louder when there is silence

I usually to avoid chaos dramas and violence

Vibing alone along with the music

A hot cup of coffee , makes me feel euphoric

I don't need anyone's company to accomplish

I love myself for what i am

An independent wallflower, who doesn't need a hand

-Anushka Achrekar

My Site Of Solace

A place where i can go

A warm blanket with hot chocolate and freezing snow
A place where i can think and think all day long

My room is the only place where i feel comfortable and where i belong

I can be all alone even if it's for years

Knowing myself better and better , overcoming all my fears

I prefer to choose good quality of small team

Even if i don't have one standing on my own feet i can be a supreme

I listen to others and respect their opinions

Even if I am one different among common millions

-Anushka Achrekar

The Bond Between Me, Pen & Paper

I am still flickering as ever,

Getting into chaos,

Facing all the battles,

I prefer silence, is better

I have two phenomenal friends,

One is paper & the other is pen

They listen to all my sorrows & pain

Even if it is over & over again

The words which I struggle to share

A pen & a paper takes all my burden,

& makes me feel light as air

This is a bond, where I am not judged at all,

Because i have two astonishing listeners,

Who give me a hand, everytime I fall

-Anushka Achrekar

Beautiful Shades Of A Wallflower

A hard desk with the night lamp on

A wooden chair where i sit upon

Where the time flies on& on

I could just think&think, looking at the things around

Working privately on my over all skills

Being inside the four walls all alone,

How good it feels

I could walk with dignity & grace ,

All by myself

I prefer to respect others opinions & their space

I live my life being an independent woman

In the cruel world of various shades of humans

-Anushka Achrekar

Will Griffith

Will Griffith is a poet and secondary school teacher in the UK. He has been published online and in print, and has work forthcoming in Reach Poetry (Indigo Dreams), and The Chamber Magazine. He is inspired by music and the sea.

Songs Of Inference And Inexperience

I

Some favour glossy lip-sediment

layered thick over cracks

sparkling accessories

quartzite catching glimmers in the gloom

I'm consuming dread

shifting, shuffling, spoiling dread

half-digested dread, thrashing around inside

like an angry foetus

fashion me a sick-bag

a collage of brown paper made from past failures

and missed opportunities

hollowed out by self-loathing

I want plane tickets for a bathroom vacation

away from all of this

II

On arrival the miraculous amnesia

of the journey fades

hugs and kisses are delivered promptly

to you, hesitantly to me

I'm tense

stiff as a diving board

or a suicide jumper

paralysed by the distance

there is a certain allure

to the darkened edges of a shoulder

seconds of genuine warmth

speeding into permanent sleep

no-one wants to hug a board

people squint at me as if making out

something crawling in the shadows

edging into corners, out of sight

III

Pressured minutes

blink in a floodlit beam of alphas

sniffing one another out

sensing a match

in artificial light

look how different they are

a separate species

there can be no communion

where sweat accompanies

a burning itch to escape

to sprint until held

then left alone

later, I rehearse interventions

imaginatively deployed

like witty nailbombs

IV

Alcohol, you false friend

pump up my gas

lodge in my engine

make me feel that flying blind

is entirely normal

platform heels

inch above the crowd

I can see you all below

I'm zooming and crooning like jazz

in a room of monks

breathe it deep

another gin

one more wine

before the fall of man

and his eternal betrayal

V

It's morning

all invitations rejected

even my mirror's overtures

are shunned

dim memories of the night before

play back like scenes

shot on cheap reel

held together

with old tape

familiar aching

at the back of my head

catching the sun

too hot

too early

left eye twitches in time

with a lesson unlearned

VI

Travelling alone on the train means

a slow drip of confused stares

intensifying at each station

flow and evaporation

in circular motion

like perspiration

on a window

ah, I'm expert

in awkwardness

I can sit with the talkers

avoid eye contact

pretend to nod off

I'm good

as the train pulls in

I cling to my bag like it might run

embracing it in a false sleep

VII

It was a gruelling trek

up the hill to the

cabin of answers

some kind of guru

big on insta

fusing transpersonal psychology

with advaita vedanta

I'm telling you,

I was desperate

humidity pressed

into my body, dripping

off the walls of narrow veins

By the time I stepped

over the threshold

I was swimming

no way back

VIII

He told me to write

told me poetry works to disorder

what order starves

I have been compulsively disordered

for three months, hoping

beyond hope

that this writing-cure

does not drip out

through the ears

onto the rug

the damp stain

of a forgotten hobby

fading with the rest

IX

Disorder

what order

starves

think on

that

barrel headlong into

the Dionysian

smash up Apollo

trample him underfoot

everything decays

people

parties

fear

X

I identify as a wallflower

my pronouns aren't

for sale

I'm comfortable

in my discomfort

orderly in my disorder

loquacious in my silence

what I have left is

time

absence of time

and petals gliding gently

where they will

in and out of your conversation

as silk slides over a warm night

Sony Sehgal

Sony Sehgal is discovering the writer and poet in herself, 25 year old. She loves to hues her blank diary pages with shades of unexpressed emotions

BARBED WIRE

A barbed cloud appeared on the sky.

Aafaaq, along the gust of confidence, blurted " Abbu, I have made my decision. The dingy old library will be converted into posh café." "Aafaaq miya, it belongs to your Nanu, his only belonging gifted to you. Think again!", his father calmly stated.

"No way! It belongs to my father, who is in heaven. No Aafaaq!", requested the tear-eyed mother. "Oh Ammi! Aap bhi na! It's going to be café, called 'Sarhad Café' Believe me, I am going to earn a lot" saying that, he stomped outside the house. He was gifted and had inherited his maternal grandpa's old library built in 1933, situated at Lahore, Pakistan. After partition, the pain for his Nanu was unbearable. Disheartened, in his gloom, he closed the library on October, 1947. For many years, nobody opened the library, few months back before the death, Nanu gifted his library to Aafaaq, which he now thinks is useless.

Aafaaq always wanted to begin his own café and now he had the place already. He was attached to his Nanu but never the library. He found it obnoxious to go in library. As the world was transforming into digital age, he felt library as the only place, where hardly anyone would cherish.

Aafaaq drove to Anarkali Bazaar, kept honking near Aamna's house. Aamna was Aafaaq's fiancée. Smoothing her lavender sharara, slipping into her jutti, she ran towards gate. Her anklets tinkled, throughout her house. Aamna smelled like trail of lavender from the orchids.

"Aafaaq! Will you stop honking? It looks rude and disrespectful. At least, you can give a call", Aamna scolded.

"Aamna Jaan! If your chattering is finished, will you ride with me?", Aafaaq teased.

"It's not chattering. And yes, I am eager to go inside your Nanujaan's library", she spoke.

Sitting behind him, Aamna mumbled a prayer for their safe ride. Aafaaq rode for nearly twenty minutes, and they reached their destination.

"Whoa!! The library is so antique. Aafaaq! Why do you want café. We both can run this", giving her puppy eyes and lopsided smile, she requested. "No! No! Don't try to be adorable. End of this talk, 'Sarhad Café', only. I am tired and sick of it. Let's get rid of these old rusty books, later we will knock it down", he blurted angrily.

Aamna meekly stood aside Aafaaq, as he opened the library. In a spur of moment, spider landed on Aamna's dupatta. She hurriedly threw it on ground, and went inside to glance it. "Nanu had such old taste. Look! Only spiders visit here", Aafaaq announced.

Aamna silently strolled inside the different sections, unwarily opened Mother Courage and Her Children, a play written by Bertolt Brecht. Flipping through the pages, a yellow papered letter fell into her hands.

Curiously, she opened the letter, dated 10th July, 1947 addressed to Famir, Wagha Border.

Famir,

Return back. Ammi is at deathbed. She wants to see you. Leave battlefield, come home. And for your birthday, I am gifting this book too.

Your sister,

Nur

Folding the letter, gently Aamna placed back in the book. Her heart began pondering on whether did Famir receive this letter or not. "How come this gifted book is in the library?", holding her breath, she asked.

Aafaaq, sighed and then spoke, "Some undelivered books were directly sent here. Why?"

Silently, she handed the book to him along the letter. Absentmindedly, she went back and picked another book called Diwan-e-Ghalib a famous poetry book written by the famous Persian and Urdu poet, Mirza Asadullah Khan

Ghalib. A letter again appeared again, dated on 14 February, 1947, addressing to Swarna

Dear Swarna,

Today, please arrive in the park, in your area. And wear pink salwar kameez, my favourite. I know situation is worse, but I am there for you. Lovingly, keeping this letter, in between this ghazals. Dream of me...

Your,
Rajan

"Did she met Rajan?", Aamna shouted in horror. Aafaaq standing near her asked, "Did Famir meet his dying mother?".

Both were dumbfounded for a moment. "Did you realise, these letters were never delivered but stayed inside the library, waiting", Aamna mumbled.

Aafaaq slowly spoke, "During the violence of Partition, many failed to receive the books as I recount, Nanu informed me. This is dreadful, to be waiting for these letters."

"Earlier, I guess people would have secretly communicated by sliding letters into books. Hey Aafaaq, let's search for more letters.", meekly she decided.

Aafaaq went into spiritual section. He randomly searched in between few books, and there came another letter. Dated on 10th August, 1947, addressing to Zara Khan.

Dear Zara,

My family has decided to go in Sangrur, Punjab. Come with me, nobody will ever tear us apart. I will cherish and respect you and your beautiful soul. Religion is pious and truly gifted, which I will never object. My servant has agreed to deliver this letter to you, hiding in one of the spiritual book. Please come tomorrow in the station at 10 a.m. I will be waiting.

Love,
Veer

The book slopped in the floor, Aafaaq covered his eyes. Hearing his soft cry, Aamna hurriedly gave him a hug, continuously asking his reason of crying.

"Zara never received this letter"

"What?", Aamna asked.

Closing his eyes, he said, "Nanu shared this story with me. Veer's servant did take this book to deliver the letter, but reaching there, he found that Zara's family was brutally butchered hours back, in gust of Partition. The servant unaware of it, returned book in the library." "Shit! Veer kept waiting for her."

Reading the letter, Aamna shed few tears.

They both were hardly aware, that Partition had made lives of people so miserable. They felt like the library was echoing the noise of several hearts. Aamna found few train tickets to Lucknow, unaware whether anybody used them. Few books had blood stain, which Nanu searched and brought back in library, from blood hounded railway stations.

Aafaaq and Aamna went back searching more undelivered letters in between the books. Hardly anyone knew 'A single barbed wire declared Partition', left this letters lying between the waiting hearts.

- Sony Sehgal

LEFT OVER HEARTBEATS.

Often wondered,
how could that
be possible

Over the years
anonymous;
in a known path.
it's broken,
shattered;
beyond repair.

Yet it keeps
on going now.

Over the cup
of a dead tea
along;
cheerless chores.

Showered and
dressed.
With a
phony expression,
pseudo walk,
to a spot.

But
deep inside,
a part of
you
had died;
With the
Leftover Heartbeats...

- Sony Sehgal

BLOTTED INK

Some commented, that;
Weed resulted his aloofness
While others stated;
Alcohol dissolved him detached,
may be the Smoke was the reason
of his exile;
Or his obesity
that withdrawed him from people,
Or else the single relationship status;
resulted in beleagured.

Hardly any soul noticed
His solitariness was the reason
of blotted ink :
in crumbled diary pages

- Sony Sehgal

Manpreet Singh

Manpreet Singh is an emerging writer. Manpreet holds a Bachelor of Arts degree. He is also a good listener and reads books related to Punjabi literature. He used to write poetry and stories in his college days. He enjoys pursuing this hobby during freehours.

ਇੱਛਾਵਾਂ

ਪਤਾ ਨਹੀਂ ਕੀ ਹਨ ਇੱਛਾਵਾਂ ਮੇਰੀਆਂ?
ਜੋ ਪੱਥਰ ਤੇ ਲਕੀਰ ਨਹੀਂ ਬਣਦੀਆਂ।
ਇੱਛਾਵਾਂ ਦੀ ਅਸਥਿਰਤਾ ਹੀ
ਮਨ ਦੀਆਂ ਸਭੇ ਸਦਰਾਂ ਨੂੰ ਠੱਗਦੀ
ਹਰ ਵੇਲੇ ਇਹਨਾਂ ਦੀ ਪੂਰਤੀ ਲਈ
ਉਹ ਸਭ ਕਰਦਾ
ਜੋ ਕਦੇ ਨਹੀਂ ਕੀਤਾ।
ਉਪਜਿਆ ਮਨ ਦਾ ਚਾਅ ਵੀ
ਸਦਾ ਛੂਠ ਪੈਂਦਾ
ਕਿ,ਹੁਣ ਤੋਂ ਮੈਂ ਕੋਈ ਇੱਛਾ ਨਹੀਂ ਰੱਖਣੀ
ਪਰ ਫਿਰ ਤੋਂ ਉਹ ਹੀ ਅੰਦਰੂਨੀ ਚਾਹਤ
ਸਭ ਕੁੱਝ ਪਾਉਣ ਦੀ ਜਾਗ ਉੱਠਦੀ
ਤੇ
ਅੰਦਰੋਂ ਅੰਦਰੀਂ ਹੱਡਾਂ ਨੂੰ ਠਾਰਦੀ
ਕਿਸੇ ਦਿੱਤੇ ਕੰਮ ਨੂੰ ਪੂਰਾ ਕਰਨ ਲਈ
ਕਾਮਾ ਬਣਾਉਂਦੀ
ਤੇ
ਮਿੱਟੀ ਦਾ ਬੁੱਤ ਸਿਰਫ਼ ਇੱਕ ਇਸ਼ਾਰੇ ਤੇ ਨੱਚਣ ਲੱਗ ਜਾਂਦਾ
ਆਪਣੀ ਅਸਥਾਈ ਪ੍ਰਾਪਤੀ ਲਈ।
ਪਰ ਅਸਲ 'ਚ ਮਿਟਣ ਦੀ ਹੱਦ ਤਾਂ ਮੇਰੀ ਏ
ਇਹਨਾਂ ਨੇ ਕਦ ਮਿੱਟਣਾ
ਸਗੋਂ, ਸਾਹਾਂ ਦੇ ਨਾਲ਼ ਨਾਲ਼ ਉਮਰਾਂ ਦੇ ਪੈਂਡੇ ਤੱਕ

ਵੱਧਦੀਆਂ ਹੀ ਜਾਣੀਆਂ
ਇੱਛਾਵਾਂ ਮੇਰੀਆਂ।

ਮਨਪ੍ਰੀਤ ਸਿੰਘ ਜਨਾਗਲ

ਪਲੀਤਣ

ਹੁਣ ਸਭ ਕੁੱਝ ਪਲੀਤ ਹੈ
ਮੇਰਾ ਯਕੀਨ ਕਰ
ਉਹ ਥਾਂ ਅਪਵਿੱਤਰ ਹੋ ਚੁੱਕੀ ਹੈ
ਜਿੱਥੇ ਤੂੰ ਸੀ
ਜਿੱਥੇ ਤੈਨੂੰ ਲਕੋ ਰੱਖਿਆ ਹੋਇਆ ਸੀ
ਜਿੱਥੇ ਤੈਨੂੰ ਮੇਰੇ ਸਿਵਾ ਕੋਈ ਨਹੀਂ ਸੀ ਦੇਖ਼ ਸਕਦਾ
ਹੁਣ ਬਹੁਤ ਹੀ ਅਸਹਿਣਸ਼ੀਲ
ਬੇ-ਬਸ ਤੇ
ਯਤਨਹੀਣ ਹੋ ਗਿਆ ਹਾਂ
ਹੁਣ ਨਿੱਕੀ-ਨਿੱਕੀ ਗੱਲ
ਖੋਪੜ੍ਹ ਨੂੰ ਗਰਮ ਕਰ ਦਿੰਦੀ ਹੈ
ਆਪਣੇ ਆਪ ਨਾਲ਼ ਹੀ
ਰੁੱਸਿਆ-ਰੁੱਸਿਆ ਹੋਇਆ
ਰਹਿਣ ਲੱਗ ਪਿਆ ਹਾਂ
ਹੁਣ ਇੱਕ ਥਾਵੇਂ ਹੀ
ਨਿਗ੍ਹਾ ਟਿਕੀ ਰਹਿੰਦੀ ਹੈ
ਬੇ-ਸੁਧ ਹੋਇਆ ਪਿਆ ਹਾਂ
ਹੁਣ ਇੱਕ ਹਾਕ ਤੇ ਨਹੀਂ
ਕਈ ਹਾਕਾਂ ਧਿਆਨ ਚ ਜੋੜਦੀਆਂ ਨੇ
ਅੱਖਾਂ ਬੰਦ ਰਹਿਣਾ ਪਸੰਦ ਕਰਦੀਆਂ ਨੇ
ਪਿੱਠ ਖੜਨਾ ਨਹੀਂ ਚਾਹੁੰਦੀ
ਪੈਰ ਤੁਰਨਾ ਨਹੀਂ ਚਾਹੁੰਦੇ
ਇਵੇਂ ਲੱਗਦਾ ਜਿਵੇਂ ਜ਼ਿੰਦਗੀ ਬੇ-ਰੰਗ ਹੈ
ਜਿਵੇਂ ਪੂਰਾ ਬ੍ਰਹਿਮੰਡ ਖੜ੍ਹ ਗਿਆ ਹੋਵੇ
ਇੱਕ ਮਨ ਦੀ ਪਵਿੱਤਰਤਾ ਭੰਗ ਹੋਣ ਨਾਲ

ਏਨੀ ਉਥਲ-ਪੁਥਲ
ਬਹੁਤ ਭਾਰੀ ਨੁਕਸਾਨ ਹੋ ਗਿਆ ਹੈ
ਰੂਹ ਦੇ ਹਰ ਤਿਣਕੇ ਦਾ
ਕੱਲ੍ਹਾ-ਕੱਲ੍ਹਾ ਅੰਗ ਬੇ-ਹਰਕਤ ਹੋ ਗਿਆ ਹੈ
ਸੱਚੀ ਇੱਕ ਇਕੱਲੀ ਰੂਹ
ਨਾ-ਪਾਕ ਹੋਣ ਨਾਲ
ਇਕੱਲੇ ਮਨ ਦੇ ਅਸ਼ਾਂਤ ਹੋਣ ਨਾਲ
ਮਨ ਅੰਦਰ ਤੇਰੀ ਹੋਂਦ ਨਾ ਹੋਣ ਨਾਲ
ਪਰ ਰੂਹ ਇਹ ਸਭ ਝੱਲ ਕੇ ਵੀ
ਆਖ ਰਹੀ ਹੈ ਕਿ
ਬਾਹਰੀ ਸਾਰੀ ਸਜਾਵਟ ਸਿਰਫ਼ ਸਿਫ਼ਰ ਹੈ
ਪੂਰੀ ਕਾਇਨਾਤ ਦੇ ਰੰਗ ਤਾਂ
ਮਨ ਦੀ ਅੰਦਰੂਨੀ
ਪਵਿੱਤਰਤਾ ਸੰਗ ਪੱਕੇ ਪਏ ਹਨ
ਜਿਹੜੇ ਕਦੇ ਨਹੀਂ ਮਿਟਦੇ।

ਮਨਪ੍ਰੀਤ ਸਿੰਘ ਜਨਾਗਲ

ਰੱਜ

ਰੱਜ ਭਾਂਤ ਭਾਂਤ ਦਾ
ਰੱਜ ਤਾਂ ਰੱਜ ਰੱਜ ਹੈ
ਰੱਜ ਨਾ ਹੱਦਾਂ ਵਿੱਚ
ਤਦ ਪੱਕੀ ਮਿੱਥ ਨਾ

ਗੱਲ ਮਨ ਭਰਨ ਦੀ
ਰੱਜ ਛੇਤੀ ਆਉਂਦਾ
ਰੱਜ ਸਾਂਝ ਵਧਾਵੇ
ਫਿਰ ਝੁਰੜੀਆਂ ਪਾਉਂਦਾ

ਰੱਜ ਰਿਸ਼ਤੇ ਤੋੜ੍ਹੇ
ਤਦ ਖ਼ੂਨ ਹੈ ਡੁੱਲ੍ਹਦਾ
ਰੱਜ ਹਿੰਮਤੀ ਬਣਕੇ
ਘਰ ਘਰ ਵਿੱਚ ਘੁੰਮਦਾ

ਰੱਜ ਪਾ ਕਾਲ਼ੇ ਕੱਪੜੇ
ਵਿੱਚ ਭੇਸ ਦੇ ਲੁੱਕਦਾ
ਅੱਜ ਮਤਲਬੀ ਬਣਕੇ
ਫਰਜ਼ ਲਾ ਲਾ ਸੁੱਟਦਾ

ਰੱਜ ਰੂਹ ਦਾ ਹਾਣੀ
ਹਰ ਪਾਸੇ ਦਿੱਸਦਾ
ਕੋਈ ਗੰਢ ਪਿਆਰ ਦੀ
ਨਾ ਪਾਉਂਦਾ ਦਿੱਸਦਾ

ਰੱਜ ਕਾਮਾ ਸਿਰਜੇ
ਰਤਾ ਝੂਠ ਨਾ ਲੱਗਦਾ

ਰੱਜ ਡਕੈਤ ਦੇ ਰਸਤੇ
ਖ਼ਵਾਇਸ਼ਾ ਨੂੰ ਲੱਭਦਾ

ਰੱਜ ਪ੍ਰਛਾਵਾਂ ਬਣ ਕੇ
ਮੇਰੇ ਨਾਲ਼ ਹੈ ਤੁਰਦਾ
ਰੱਜ ਢੋਂਗੀ ਬਣ ਕੇ
ਰੂਹ ਰੂਹ ਨੂੰ ਲੁੱਟਦਾ

ਰੱਜ ਸਮੁੰਦਰ ਨਾਮੀ
ਜੋ ਕਦੇ ਨਾ ਭਰਦਾ
ਰੱਜ ਕਦੇ ਨਾ ਆਵੇ
ਅੰਤ ਥੱਕ ਹਾਰ " ਮੈਂ " ਹੀ ਜਾਂਦਾ।

ਮਨਪ੍ਰੀਤ(ਮਨ) ਸਿੰਘ ਜਨਾਗਲ

ਮੌਤ

ਮੌਤ ਆਉਂਦੀ ਹੈ,

ਚਲੀ ਜਾਂਦੀ ਹੈ,

ਉਸਨੂੰ ਨਹੀਂ ਮਿਲਦਾ ਹਾਂ,ਕਿਉਂਕਿ

ਹਾਲੇ ਵਿਅਸਥ ਹਾਂ ਜਿਉਂਣ 'ਚ

ਫੱਟ ਸਿਉਣ ' ਚ

ਪਰ

ਇੱਕ ਨਾ ਇੱਕ ਦਿਨ,

ਘੜ੍ਹੀ,ਪਲ਼ ਫੜ੍ਹਿਆ ਜ਼ਰੂਰ ਜਾਵਾਂਗਾ।

ਜਿਸ ਦੇ ਕੋਲੋਂ

ਭੱਜ ਭੱਜ ਦੂਰ ਜਾ ਰਿਹਾ ਸਮਝਦਾ ਹਾਂ,

ਅਸਲ ਦੇ ਵਿੱਚ ਉਸਦੇ ਹੀ ਨਜ਼ਦੀਕ ਜਾ ਰਿਹਾ ਹਾਂ,

ਇਸਦਾ ਉਦੇਸ਼ ਵੀ ਤਾਂ ਇੱਕ ਹੀ ਹੈ।

ਜਿਉਣਾ ਭਟਕਣ ਹੈ,ਉਦੋਂ

ਜਦੋਂ ਆਦਮੀ ਜਿਉਂਣਾ ਨਹੀਂ ਚਾਹੁੰਦਾ,

ਮੌਤ ਸਹੀ ਰਸਤਾ ਹੈ,ਉਦੋਂ

ਜਦੋਂ ਜਹਿਨ ਇਸ ਤੋਂ ਬੇ-ਖ਼ਬਰ ਹੁੰਦਾ ਹੈ।

ਪਰ......ਸੱਚ ਇਹ ਹੈ,

ਕਿ

ਖ਼ਾਤਮਾ ਹੁਣ ਕੋਈ ਅਵਸਥਾ ਨਹੀਂ ਰਿਹਾ,

ਹੁਣ ਤਾਂ ਇਹ ਇੱਕ ਅਚਾਨਕ ਵਾਪਰਿਆ

ਅਣ-ਹੋਇਆ,ਅਣ-ਚਾਹਿਆ

ਦਰਦਨਾਕ

ਹਾਦਸਾ ਬਣ ਗਿਆ ਹੈ।

ਮਨਪ੍ਰੀਤ ਸਿੰਘ ਜਨਾਗਲ

ਰਾਤ

ਰਾਤਾਂ ਦਾ ਇੱਕ ਆੜ੍ਹੀ ਹੈ
ਰਾਤਾਂ ਦੀ ਚੁੱਪ ਲਾੜ੍ਹੀ ਹੈ
ਰਾਤਾਂ ਦੀ ਬਾਤ ਕਰਦੀ
ਰਾਤਾਂ ਨੇ ਧੁੱਪ ਸਾੜ੍ਹੀ ਹੈ
ਰਾਤ ਦਾ ਸ਼ੋਰ ਸੁਣੀ
ਰਾਤ ਨੂੰ ਇੱਕ ਯਾਦ ਬੁਣੀ
ਰਾਤ ਹੀ ਇਕੱਲ ਹੈ
ਰਾਤ ਦੀ ਹੈ ਰਾਤ ਹੁਣੀ
ਰਾਤ ਬੁੱਝ ਕੀ ਹੈ?
ਰਾਤ ਰੱਤ ਕੀ ਹੈ?
ਰਾਤ ਦਾ ਆਗਾਜ਼ ਕਦੋਂ?
ਰਾਤ ਅੰਤ ਕੀ ਹੈ?
ਰਾਤ ਖ਼ੁਦ ਨਾਲ ਯਾਰੀ
ਰਾਤ ਦੀ ਹੈ ਗੱਲ ਸਾਰੀ
ਰਾਤ ਦਾ ਟਿਕਾ ਅਲੱਗ
ਰਾਤ ਨੂੰ ਨਿਗ੍ਹਾ ਮਾਰੀ
ਰਾਤ ਬੋਲੇ ਦਿਨ ਸਾਰਾ
ਰਾਤ ਨੱਚੇ ਹਰ ਤਾਰਾ
ਰਾਤ ਦਾ ਸੂਰਜ ਠੰਡਾ
ਰਾਤ ਬਾਤ ਇੱਕੋ ਚਾਰਾ
ਰਾਤ ਬੱਦਲ ਆੜ੍ਹੀ ਬੋਲਣ
ਰਾਤ ਦੀ ਨਾ ਗੁੱਥੀ ਖੋਲ੍ਹਣ
ਰਾਤ ਦੇ ਦੁੱਖ ਚੰਨ ਜਾਣਦਾ
ਰਾਤ ਨੂੰ ਕੋਈ ਹੋਰ ਨਾ ਫੋਲ੍ਹਣ।

ਮਨਪ੍ਰੀਤ ਸਿੰਘ ਜਨਾਗਲ

ਚਣੌਤੀ

ਦੁੱਖਾਂ 'ਚ,ਦਿੱਕਤਾਂ 'ਚ,ਹੱਸਣਾ, ਚਣੌਤੀ ਹੈ
ਜ਼ਿੰਦਗੀ ਦੇ ਮਾੜੇ ਦੌਰ ਨੂੰ
ਹਾਂ, ਚਣੌਤੀ ਹੈ
ਚੱਲਦੇ ਸਾਹਾਂ 'ਚ ਠੱਗੀਆਂ ਦੇ ਭੌਰ ਨੂੰ
ਚਣੌਤੀ ਨਹੀਂ ਮੰਨਦੀ ਕਾਲੇ ਕਲੂਟੇ ਦੇ ਟਿੱਕਿਆ ਨੂੰ
ਨਹੀਂ ਮੰਨਦੀ,ਕਿ ਅੱਖ ਭੰਨ੍ਹਦੀ ਮੱਥੇ ਦੇ ਸਿੱਕਿਆਂ ਨੂੰ
ਚਣੌਤੀ ਮੰਨਦੀ ਹੈ,ਬੰਦੇ ਦੇ ਸਬਰਾਂ ਨੂੰ
ਦੁੱਖਾਂ ਨਾਲ ਲੜ੍ਹਨ ਵਾਲੇ ਦੇ ਜ਼ਬਰਾਂ ਨੂੰ।

ਮਨਪ੍ਰੀਤ ਸਿੰਘ ਜਨਾਗਲ

ਕੰਮੀ

ਕੰਮੀਆਂ ਨੂੰ ਕਦੇ ਵੀ ਸੁਣਿਆ ਨਹੀਂ ਜਾਂਦਾ
ਹਮੇਸ਼ਾ ਵਾਹਿਆ ਹੀ ਜਾਂਦਾ
ਤੱਪਦੇ ਤੱਤੇ ਤੱਵੇ ਵਰਗਿਆਂ ਬੱਠਲਾਂ ਨਾਲ
ਮੋਮੀ ਨਰਮ ਸਿਰਾਂ ਤੇ ਗੰਜਾਂਪਣ ਪਾਇਆ ਜਾਂਦਾ
ਮਜ਼ਬੂਰੀਆਂ ਬੁਢਾਪੇ ਨੂੰ ਵੀ ਮਜ਼ਦੂਰ ਬਣਾਈ ਰੱਖਦੀਆਂ
ਔਲਾਦਾ ਨੂੰ ਤਾਂ ਬਸ ਵਾਰਿਸ ਬਣਾਇਆ ਜਾਂਦਾ
ਕਮੀਆਂ ਸਭ ਦੇ ਵਿੱਚ ਵਾਧੂ ਹੁੰਦੀਆਂ
ਪਰ ਵਾਧੇ ਨੂੰ ਕਦੇ ਘਟਾਇਆ ਨਹੀਂ ਜਾਂਦਾ
ਚਮੜ੍ਹੀ ਨੂੰ ਜਿਉਂਦਾ ਰੱਖਣਾ ਬਹੁਤ ਔਖਾ,ਬਸ
ਇੰਝ ਸਮਝੋ ਕਿ ਚਮੜ੍ਹੀ ਦੇ ਹੀ ਛਿੱਲੜਾਂ ਨੂੰ ਲਾਹਿਆ ਜਾਂਦਾ।

ਮਨਪ੍ਰੀਤ ਸਿੰਘ ਜਨਾਗਲ

ਇੱਕ ਕੁੜੀ

ਇੱਕ ਕੁੜੀ ਗੁੰਮਨਾਮ ਹੈ।
ਮੇਰੇ ਚੇਤਿਆਂ ਦੀ ਪੋਸ਼ਾਕ ਹੈ,
ਪ੍ਰਛਾਵੇ ਵਾਂਗ ਨਾਲ ਨਾਲ ਚੱਲਦੀ,
ਉਹ ਕੁੜੀ ਸੱਚੀ ਕੁਦਰਤ ਦਾ ਸ਼ਿੰਗਾਰ ਹੈ।

....

ਬਹੁਤ ਹੀ ਸ਼ਰਮਾਕਲ ,ਚੁੱਪ ਦੀ ਜੋ ਮੂਰਤ
ਬਸ, ਉਸ ਕੁੜੀ ਨਾਲ ਮੈਨੂੰ ਪਿਆਰ ਹੈ।

ਮਨਪ੍ਰੀਤ ਸਿੰਘ ਜਨਾਗਲ

Harf Inder

His name is Harwinder Singh but the name "Harf Inder" has been given by a special friend. He holds a BSc degree in Agriculture from Punjab Agricultural University. He loves art and is always striving to uplift theartists.

ਜੇ

ਸੁਣਦਾ ਜੇ ਕਿਤੇ ਰੱਬ ਗਰੀਬਾਂ ਦੀ
ਭਿਖਾਰੀ ਬੈਠਾ ਕੋਈ ਮੰਦਰ ਦੇ ਬਾਹਰ ਨਾ ਹੁੰਦਾ।

ਦਿੱਤੀ ਜੇ ਹੁੰਦੀ ਸੂਝ-ਬੂਝ ਸਭਨਾਂ ਨੂੰ ਰੱਬ ਨੇ ,
ਬੀਰਬਲ ਵਿੱਚ ਅਕਬਰ ਦੇ ਦਰਵਾਰ ਨਾ ਹੁੰਦਾ।

ਦੱਸੋ ਫਿਰ ਕੌਣ ਬਣਾਉਂਦਾ ਮਿੱਟੀ ਤੋਂ ਖ਼ੁਦਾ ਨੂੰ ?
ਹੱਥ ਮਿੱਟੀ ਨੂੰ ਲਾਉਣ ਵਾਲਾ ਜੇ ਘੁਮਿਆਰ ਨਾ ਹੁੰਦਾ।

ਜੇ ਨਾ ਬਖ਼ਸੀ ਹੁੰਦੀ ਦਾਤ ਕਲਗੀਆਂ ਵਾਲੇ ਨੇ ,
ਦਸਤਾਰ ਨਾਲ ਦਿੱਖਦਾ ਵੱਖਰਾ ਕੋਈ ਸਰਦਾਰ ਨਾ ਹੁੰਦਾ।

ਜੇ ਮੰਨਦੇ ਮਾਪੇ ਧੀਆਂ ਨੂੰ ਪੁੱਤ ਆਪਣਾ ,
ਕਿਸੇ ਬਾਬਲ ਦੇ ਸਿਰ ਤੇ ਧੀ ਨਾਮ ਦਾ ਕੋਈ ਭਾਰ ਨਾ ਹੁੰਦਾ।

ਅੱਜ ਵੀ ਆਪਣੇ ਬੈਠ ਦੇ ਰਲਕੇ ਕੱਚੇ ਘਰਾਂ ਵਿੱਚ ,
ਜੇ ਮੁੱਕਿਆ ਦਿਲਾਂ ਵਿੱਚੋਂ ਸੱਚਾ-ਸੁੱਚਾ ਪਿਆਰ ਨਾ ਹੁੰਦਾ।

ਕਿਹਨੇ ਰੱਖਣੇ ਸੀ ਜਾਨਵਰ ਘਰਾਂ ਵਿੱਚ ਦੱਸੋ ?
ਕੁੱਤਾ ਜੇ ਆਪਣੇ ਮਾਲਿਕ ਪ੍ਰਤੀ ਵਫ਼ਾਦਾਰ ਨਾ ਹੁੰਦਾ।

ਕੀ ਲੱਗਣਾ ਸੀ ਯੁੱਧ ? ਕਿਵੇਂ ਹੋਣੀਆਂ ਸੀ ਜੰਗਾਂ ?
ਜੇ ਬਣਿਆ ਕਿਤੇ ਕੋਈ ਹਥਿਆਰ ਨਾ ਹੁੰਦਾ ।

ਕਿਵੇਂ ਫਿਰ ਵੱਜਦੀਆਂ ਰੂਹ ਤੇ ਸੱਟਾਂ " ਇੰਦਰ " ?
ਜੇ ਪਾਕ ਪਵਿੱਤਰ ਰੂਹਾਂ ਵਾਲਾ ਪਿਆਰ ਨਾ ਹੁੰਦਾ ।

ਬੜਾ ਔਖਾ ਹੈ

ਬੜਾ ਔਖਾ ਹੈ
ਕਿਸੇ ਲਈ ਖ਼ਾਸ ਹੋਣਾ।

ਲਫਜ਼ਾਂ ਤੋਂ ਵਾਂਝੇ
ਦਿਲ ਦੇ ਖਿਆਲ ਹੋਣੇ,
ਜਵਾਬਾਂ ਤੋਂ ਵਾਂਝੇ
ਕਿੰਨੇ ਹੀ ਸਵਾਲ ਹੋਣੇ,
ਬਹਿਕੇ ਨਦੀ ਕਿਨਾਰੇ
ਫਿਰ ਵੀ ਪਿਆਸ ਹੋਣਾ,
ਬੜਾ ਔਖਾ ਹੈ
ਕਿਸੇ ਲਈ ਖ਼ਾਸ ਹੋਣਾ।

ਆਪਣਿਆਂ ਵਿੱਚ ਹੀ
ਬੁੱਤ ਹੋ ਜਾਣਾ,
ਬਹਾਰਾਂ ਵਿੱਚ ਹੀ
ਪੱਤਝੜ ਰੁੱਤ ਹੋ ਜਾਣਾ,
ਸਾਹਾਂ ਦਾ ਚੱਲਦੇ ਰਹਿਣਾ
ਜ਼ਿਸਮ ਦਾ ਲਾਸ ਹੋਣਾ,
ਬੜਾ ਔਖਾ ਹੈ
ਕਿਸੇ ਲਈ ਖ਼ਾਸ ਹੋਣਾ।

ਬੁੱਲਾਂ ਤੇ ਹਾਸੇ
ਦਿਲ ਚ ਗਮੀ ਹੋਣਾ,
ਸੱਭ ਹੁੰਦੇ ਵੀ
ਕਿਸੇ ਦੀ ਕਮੀ ਹੋਣਾ,
ਜ਼ਿਸਮ ਤੋਂ ਦੂਰ
ਦਿਲ ਦੇ ਪਾਸ ਹੋਣਾ,

ਬੜਾ ਔਖਾ ਹੈ
ਕਿਸੇ ਲਈ ਖ਼ਾਸ ਹੋਣਾ।

ਜਿਸਨੇ ਆਉਣਾ ਨਹੀਂ
ਉਸਦੀ ਉਡੀਕ ਹੋਣਾ,
ਦਿਲ ਦਾ ਕਬਰ
ਚੁੱਪ ਦਾ ਚੀਕ ਹੋਣਾ,
ਹੋ ਸੱਚ ਤੋਂ ਵਾਕਿਫ਼
ਫਿਰ ਵੀ ਆਸ ਹੋਣਾ,
ਬੜਾ ਔਖਾ ਹੈ
ਕਿਸੇ ਲਈ ਖ਼ਾਸ ਹੋਣਾ।

ਰਿਸ਼ਤੇ

ਰਿਸ਼ਤੇ ਰਬੜ ਦੀ ਤਰਾਂ ਹੁੰਦੇ ਨੇ

ਇਹਨਾਂ ਨੂੰ ਜਿੰਨ੍ਹਾਂ ਵੱਡਾ ਕਰਕੇ ਛੱਡ ਦੇ ਹਾਂ
ਓਨੀਂ ਹੀ ਡੂੰਗੀ ਸੱਟ ਮਾਰਦੇ ਨੇ।

" ਮੁਹੱਬਤ "

ਮੁਹੱਬਤ ਦੀ ਅੱਗ ਵਿੱਚ ਹੀ ਮਹਿਫੂਜ਼ ਹਾਂ ਮੈਂ
ਬੇਵਫ਼ਾਈ ਦੀ ਛਾਂ ਵੀ ਪਈ ਤੇ ਸੜ੍ਹ ਜਾਵਾਂਗਾ।

" ਸਿੰਗਾਰ "

ਸ਼ਬਦ ਮੋਤੀ ਤੇ ਕਵਿਤਾ ਮਾਲਾ ਹੈ
ਤੈਨੂੰ ਸਾਮ੍ਹਣੇ ਬਿਠਾਕੇ ,

ਮੈਂ ਤੇਰਾ ਸਿੰਗਾਰ ਕਰਨਾ ਹੈ।

ਸਫ਼ਰ-ਏ-ਜ਼ਿੰਦਗੀ

ਕੈਸੀ ਇਹ ਖਿਜ਼ਾ ਦੀ ਰੁੱਤ ਹੈ
ਤੇ ਮੌਸਮ ਹੈ ਬੇਜ਼ਾਰਾਂ ਦਾ
ਰੂਹ ਤਾਂ ਇਕੱਲੀ ਚੀਕਾਂ ਮਾਰੇ
ਭਾਵੇਂ ਦੇਹ ਨੂੰ ਸਾਥ ਹਜ਼ਾਰਾਂ ਦਾ।

ਨਾ ਰੱਖ ਅਜਾਬ ਦਾ ਹਰਾਸ ਕੋਈ
ਮੌਲਾ ਨਾਲ ਰੱਖ ਸੀਰ ਪਾਕੇ
ਖਿਜਾ ਦੀ ਰੁੱਤ ਵੀ ਮੁਕੇਗੀ
ਆਵੇਗਾ ਮੌਸਮ ਪਿਆਰਾਂ ਦਾ।

ਪਵਨ ਵੀ ਤੇਰੇ ਵੱਲ ਦੀ ਹੋਣੀ
ਖੁਸ਼ਬੂ ਦੀ ਤਰ੍ਹਾਂ ਫੈਲ ਜਾਣਾ
ਜੱਦ ਉਡਣਾ ਤੂੰ ਵਾਂਗ ਉਕਾਬ ਦੇ
ਹੰਕਾਰ ਨਾ ਰਹਿਣਾ ਪਹਾੜਾਂ ਦਾ।

ਖਿਆਨਤ ਨਾ ਬਣ ਜਾਵੀਂ
ਮੁਹਤਾਜ ਰਹੀਂ ਉਸ ਮਾਲਿਕ ਦਾ
ਜ਼ਹੂਰ ਹੋਣੀ ਤੇਰੀਆਂ ਅੱਖਾਂ ਵਿੱਚ
ਰੰਗ ਫਿੱਕਾ ਲੱਗਣਾ ਬਜ਼ਾਰਾਂ ਦਾ।

ਹਿਜ਼ਰ

ਚਾਨਣ ਦੀ ਵੈਰਨ ਨਾਲ ਲਾ ਯਾਰੀ ਮੈਂ ਭੁੰਜੇ ਸੀ ਮੱਲੇ ,
ਦਰਦ , ਤਨਹਾਈ ਨੂੰ ਗਲ ਸੀ ਮੈਂ ਲਾਇਆ ਹੰਝੂ ਸੀ ਕੱਲੇ ।

ਪਤਝੜ ਰੁੱਤੇ ਝੱੜਗੇ ਸੀ ਪੱਤੇ ਤਾਂ ਵੀ ਅਮੀਰੀ ਸੀ ਕੋਲ ,
ਬਹਾਰ ਰੁੱਤੇ ਰੌਣਕ ਸੀ ਆਈ ਕੱਖ ਨਾ ਸੀ ਮੇਰੇ ਪੱਲੇ ।

ਕੁਝ ਸਿੱਕੇ ਟਕਸਾਲੀ , ਕੁੱਝ ਹਿਜ਼ਰ ਦੀ ਅੱਗੇ ਤਪਾਏ ਸੀ ਮੈਂ ,
ਮੁਸੀਬਤ ਸੀ ਸਿਰ 'ਤੇ ਖੋਟੇ ਓਹ ਸਿੱਕੇ ਨਾ ਚਲੇ ।

ਪੁਸ਼ਾਕ ਯਕੀਨ ਵਾਲੀ ਕਰ ਲੀਰੋ-ਲੀਰ ,ਹਥਿਆਰ ਸੀ ਚੁੱਕੇ ,
ਲੂਣ ਸੀ ਭੁਕਿਆ ਜਦ ਮੇਰੇ ਜ਼ਖਮ ਸੀ ਅੱਲੇ ।

ਨਿੱਕਾ ਸੀ ਮਖ਼ਮਲ ਦੀ ਚਾਦਰ ਤੇ ਸੌਂਦਾ ਸੀ ਮੈਂ ,
ਅੰਤਾਂ ਦਾ ਜਦ ਸੀ ਵੇਲਾ ਆਇਆ ਕੰਡੇ ਸੀ ਥੱਲੇ ।

ਉਹ ਚਿਹਰਾ

ਮੈਂ ਜਿਸਨੂੰ ਭੁੱਲ ਨਹੀਂ ਸਕਦਾ,
ਬਿਨਾ ਜਿਸਦੇ
ਕਿਸੇ ਤੇ ਡੁੱਲ੍ਹ ਨਹੀਂ ਸਕਦਾ,
ਅੱਖ ਮੇਰੀ ਦਾ ਕਰਾਰ ਹੈ ਉਹ ਚਿਹਰਾ,
ਰੂਹ ਮੇਰੀ ਦਾ ਪਿਆਰ ਹੈ ਉਹ ਚਿਹਰਾ,
ਦਿਲ ਵਿੱਚ ਵਾਸ ਹੈ ਉਸਦਾ
ਜਿਸਮਾਂ ਤੋਂ ਦੂਰ ਹੈ ਉਹ ਚਿਹਰਾ,
ਚਾਹ ਕੇ ਵੀ ਨਹੀਂ ਹੋ ਸਕਦਾ ਮੇਰਾ
ਬੜਾ ਮਜਬੂਰ ਹੈ ਉਹ ਚਿਹਰਾ,
ਮੇਰੀ ਅੱਖ ਨੂੰ ਦੀਦ ਵੀ ਨਹੀਂ ਦਿੰਦਾ
ਬੜਾ ਮਗਰੂਰ ਹੈ ਉਹ ਚਿਹਰਾ,
ਚਰਚੇ ਨੇ ਹਰ ਜੁਬਾਨ ਤੇ
ਉਸਦੇ ਕਿ ਬੜਾ ਮਸ਼ਹੂਰ ਹੈ ਉਹ ਚਿਹਰਾ,
ਹੋਸ਼ ਨਹੀਂ ਰਹਿੰਦਾ ਕਿ
ਭੁੱਲ ਜਾਂਦਾ ਖੁੱਦ ਨੂੰ ਵੀ ਮੈ
ਮੇਰਾ ਫਿਤੂਰ ਹੈ ਉਹ ਚਿਹਰਾ,
ਮੈਂ ਪੀਂਦਾ ਹੀ ਨਹੀਂ
ਤਾਂ ਵੀ ਲੋਰ ਵਿੱਚ ਰਹਿੰਦਾ ਹਾਂ
ਕਿ ਚੜ੍ਹਿਆ ਸਰੂਰ ਹੈ ਉਹ ਚਿਹਰਾ,
ਲੱਖ ਦੇਵੇ ਦਿਲ ਤੇ ਸੱਟਾਂ
ਕਿ ਗੁਲਾਮ ਕਰ ਲਵੇ ਮੈਨੂੰ
ਫਿਰ ਵੀ ਆਖ਼ਰੀ ਸਾਹ ਤੱਕ
ਮਨਜ਼ੂਰ ਹੈ ਉਹ ਚਿਹਰਾ।

ਜ਼ਿੰਦਗੀ

ਢਿੱਡ ਨੂੰ ਗੰਢਾਂ ਦਿੱਤੀਆਂ ਨੇ,
ਭੁੱਖਾਂ ਵੀ ਭੁੱਖੀਆਂ ਮਾਰੀਆਂ ਨੇ,
ਵਕਤਾਂ ਤੋਂ ਸੱਟਾਂ ਖਾਈਆਂ ਨੇ,
ਪੀ ਪਾਣੀ ਰਾਤਾਂ ਗੁਜ਼ਾਰੀਆਂ ਨੇ।

ਅੱਖਾਂ ਨਾਲ ਵੀ ਸਮਝੌਤੇ ਹੋਏ ਨੇ,
ਨੀਂਦਾਂ ਨਿਲਾਮ ਕੀਤੀਆਂ ਨੇ,
ਦੁੱਖਾਂ ਦੀਆਂ ਕਾਲੀਆਂ ਰਾਤਾਂ ਵਿੱਚ,
ਪ੍ਰਭਾਤਾਂ ਨੂੰ ਆਵਾਜ਼ਾਂ ਮਾਰੀਆਂ ਨੇ।

ਬੜੇ ਤਰਲੇ ਕੱਢੇ ਕਿਸਮਤ ਦੇ,
ਹਰ ਪੈਰ ਜਿਹਨੇ ਅਜਮਾਇਆ ਏ,
ਲੋਕ ਪਿੰਡੇ ਤੇ ਦੁੱਖ ਹੰਢਾਉਂਦੇ ਨੇ,
ਮੈਂ ਰੂਹ ਤੇ ਸੱਟਾਂ ਸਹਾਰੀਆਂ ਨੇ।

ਮੈਂ ਆਪਣੀਆਂ ਸੱਧਰਾਂ ਮਾਰੀਆਂ ਨੇ,
ਬਾਪੂ ਦੀਆਂ ਰੀਝਾਂ ਪਿਆਰੀਆਂ ਨੇ,
ਮਿਹਨਤਾਂ ਨੂੰ ਹੁਣ ਬੂਰ ਪੈਣਾ,
ਹੰਜੂਆਂ ਨਾਲ ਸਿੰਜੀਆਂ ਕਿਆਰੀਆਂ ਨੇ।

ਮੈਂ ਮਾਂ ਨੂੰ ਸੱਜਦਾ ਕਰਦਾ ਹਾਂ,
ਸੱਭ ਪੈਰਾਂ ਵਿੱਚ ਓਹਦੇ ਧਰਦਾ ਹਾਂ,
ਓਹਨੇ ਮੋਢੇ ਚੁੱਕ ਕੇ ਰੱਖੀਆਂ ਨੇ,
ਮੇਰੇ ਫਿਕਰਾਂ ਦੀਆਂ ਭੰਡਾਂ ਭਾਰੀਆਂ ਨੇ।

ਸੋਚ

ਹੌਂਸਲੇ ਬੁਲੰਦ ਰੱਖੀਂ ,
ਜਜ਼ਬਾਤ ਕਲਮਬੰਦ ਰੱਖੀਂ ,
ਵੱਖਰੀ ਦੁਨੀਆ ਤੋਂ ਪਸੰਦ ਰੱਖੀਂ ,
ਕਰਕੇ ਦੁਨੀਆ ਨੂੰ ਦੰਗ ਰੱਖੀਂ ,
ਉੱਚੇ ਤੋਂ ਨੀਵੇਂ ਨਾਲ ਸੰਬੰਧ ਰੱਖੀਂ ,
ਗੁਰੂ ਦਾ ਬਣਕੇ ਰਹੀਂ " ਇੰਦਰ ",
ਮਨ ਨੂੰ ਆਪਣੇ ਅਹਿਸਾਨਮੰਦ ਰੱਖੀਂ,
ਬੁਰੇ ਵਕ਼ਤ ਨਾ ਡੋਲ ਜਾਵੀਂ ,
ਦਿਲ ਨੂੰ ਰਜ਼ਾਮੰਦ ਰੱਖੀਂ ,
ਉੱਡਣਾ ਵੀ ਸਿੱਖ ਜਾਣਾ ਤੂੰ ,
ਖਿਲਾਰਕੇ ਆਪਣੇ ਖੰਭ ਰੱਖੀਂ ,
ਗੁਰੂ ਦੇ ਰਹੀਂ ਲੜ ਲੱਗਕੇ ,
ਦਸਾਂ ਨਹੁੰਆਂ ਦਾ ਦਸਵੰਦ ਰੱਖੀਂ ,
ਕੀ ਪਤਾ ਕਦੋਂ ਮੁੱਕ ਜਾਵੇ ?
ਤੇਰੇ ਘੜੇ ਵਿਚੋਂ ਪਾਣੀ ,
" ਹਰਫ਼ "ਚਿਤਾ ਲਈ ਆਪਣੀ ,
ਲੱਕੜਾਂ ਦਾ ਕਰਕੇ ਪ੍ਰਬੰਧ ਰੱਖੀਂ ।

ਦਿਲ ਦੀਆਂ ਗੱਲਾਂ

ਜੋ ਦਿਲ ਦੇ ਲੁੱਚੇ ਮੂੰਹ ਦੇ ਸਾਊ
ਓਹਨਾ ਨਾਲੋਂ ਮੈ ਕੰਜ਼ਰ ਚੰਗਾ।

ਪਿੱਠ ਤੇ ਹੋਏ ਵਾਰ ਨਾਲੋਂ
ਸ਼ੀਨੇ ਵੱਜਿਆ ਖ਼ੰਜਰ ਚੰਗਾ।

ਰੱਤ ਮੰਗਦਾ ਜੋ ਇਨਸਾਨਾਂ ਦਾ
ਉਪਜਾਊ ਨਾਲੋਂ ਵਾਹਨ ਬੰਜ਼ਰ ਚੰਗਾ।

ਜਿੱਥੇ ਲੋਕ ਤੇ ਖ਼ੁਦਾ ਪੱਥਰ ਹੈ
ਕਿਵੇਂ ਕਹਿ ਦਵਾਂ ਉਹ ਮੰਦਿਰ ਚੰਗਾ।

ਸੂਰਤ ਨੂੰ ਕਿਉਂ ਤਵੱਜੋ ਦਵਾਂ ਮੈਂ
ਹੋਵੇ ਕੀ ਪਤਾ ਉਹਦਾ ਅੰਦਰ ਚੰਗਾ।

ਕੀ ਕਰਨਾ ਭਾਂਤ ਭਾਂਤ ਦੇ ਪਕਵਾਨਾਂ ਦਾ ?
ਜਿੱਥੇ ਰੱਜਨ ਭੁੱਖੇ ਸਾਦਾ ਉਹ ਲੰਗਰ ਚੰਗਾ।

ਜਿਸ ਘਰ ਨਾ ਹੋਵੇ ਰੀਤ ਪਿਆਰ ਦੀ
" ਹਰਫ਼ " ਐਸੇ ਘਰ ਤੋਂ ਖੰਡਰ ਚੰਗਾ।

Satkardeep Singh

Satkardeep Singh, Undergraduate student of Agriculture department in PAU Ludhiana, Fatehgarh Sahib born, raised in Ludhiana, Fashion model at day to influence people with appearance and Poet by heart in night to impress and change the world with his mindful thoughts.

सच...

सोच को बदलो सितारे बदल जायेंगे। नज़र को बदलो नज़ारे बदल जायेंगे। विचारों की कश्ती को बदलो , किनारे बदल जायेंगे। एक बार बुरे वक्त में तो आओ हुजूर सारे के सारे साहारे बदल जायेंगे।

दीप सतिकार

आपकी याद...

मैं कोई शायर नही हजूर बस अपनी सोच का अनचुहा सा भाग लिख देता हु,
मैं चांद को चांद नही तेरा नाम लिख देता हूं,
अगर यह चंद शबद आपके लिए शायरी है,
तो यह तो मैं आपकी याद मे सुभा शाम लिख देता हूं।

दीप सतिकार

ਇੱਕ ਦਿਨ...

ਮੁੱਕ ਜਾਣਾ ਇੱਕ ਦਿਨ ਸੱਜਣਾ ਬਸ ਕਬਰਾਂ ਤੱਕ ਦਾ ਸਫ਼ਰ ਐ, ਇਹ ਲਿਖਾਰੀ ਵਾਲਾ ਸਰੂਰ ਵੀ ਲਹਿ ਜਾਣਾ ਇੱਕ ਦਿਨ ਸੱਜਣਾ ਬਸ ਚਾਰ ਦਿਨਾਂ ਦਾ ਅਸਰ ਐ, ਸਭ ਕੁਝ ਲੁਟਾਤਾ ਤੇਰੇ ਉੱਤੇ ਸੱਜਣਾ ਫਿਰ ਵੀ ਜਾਪੇ ਇੰਝ ਮੇਰੇ ਦਿਲ ਨੂੰ ਜਿਵੇਂ ਰਹਿ ਗਈ ਕੋਈ ਕਸਰ ਐ,ਸਾਨੂੰ ਨਾ ਇਸ ਜਗ ਨਾਲ ਮੋਹ ਸੱਜਣਾ ਸਾਡਾ ਤਾਂ ਤੂੰ ਹੀ ਸ਼ੁਰੂਆਤ ਤੇ ਤੂੰ ਹੀ ਹਸ਼ਰ ਐ।

ਦੀਪ ਸਤਿਕਾਰ

ਚੁੱਪ...

ਸਿਖਰ ਦੁਪਿਹਰ ਸੱਜਣਾ ਸਿਰ ਤੇ ਚੜੀ ਧੁੱਪ ਐ,

ਬਾਤਾਂ ਕਰਨ ਨੂੰ ਤਾਂ ਦਿਲ ਕਰਦਾ ਸੱਜਣਾ ਪਰ

ਬੁੱਲ੍ਹਾਂ ਉੱਤੇ ਚੁੱਪ ਐ,

ਅਸੀਂ ਬੀਜ਼ ਇਸ਼ਕ ਦੇ ਬੀਜ਼ ਦਿੱਤੇ ਹੁਣ ਫੱਲ ਦੀ ਸਾਨੂੰ ਭੁੱਖ ਐ, ਸਾਡੇ ਸ਼ਾਇਰ ਦਾ ਨਾ ਕੋਈ ਮਹਿਬੂਬ

ਸੱਜਣਾ ਪਰ ਫਿਰ ਵੀ ਜ਼ਿੰਦਗੀ ਵਿਚ ਸੁੱਖ ਐ।

ਦੀਪ ਸਤਿਕਾਰ

ਮੁਸਾਫ਼ਿਰ...

ਕਿਸੇ ਮੁਸਾਫ਼ਿਰ ਵਾਂਗ ਬਸ ਤੁਰਦਾ ਜਾ ਰਿਹਾ ਹਾਂ, ਇਸ ਇਸ਼ਕ ਹਵਾ ਵਿਚ ਉੱਡ ਦਾ ਜਾ ਰਿਹਾ ਹਾਂ।
ਜਿਥੋਂ ਲੰਘਾਂ ਬਸ ਸੱਜਣਾ ਬੂਟੇ ਨਫ਼ਰਤ ਦੇ ਪੁੱਟਦਾ ਜਾ ਰਿਹਾ ਹਾਂ, ਸਾਨੂੰ ਵਿਹਲੜਾ ਨੂੰ ਨਾ ਕੰਮ ਕੋਈ
ਸੱਜਣਾ ਬਸ ਸ਼ਾਇਰੀ ਨਾਲ ਬੀਜ ਇਸ਼ਕ ਦੇ ਸੁਟਦਾ ਜਾ ਰਿਹਾ ਹਾਂ।

ਦੀਪ ਸਤਿਕਾਰ

ਤਸਵੀਰ....

ਮੈ ਨਿੱਤ ਦੇਖਦਾ ਆ ਉਹਨੂੰ ਖ਼ਾਬ ਚ,
ਜਿਸਦਾ ਜ਼ਿਕਰ ਹੁੰਦਾ ਮੇਰੀ ਹਰ ਇੱਕ ਗੱਲ ਬਾਤ ਚ,
ਸਿਰਫ ਉਹਦੀਆਂ ਹੀ ਪਾਉਂਦਾ ਬਾਤਾਂ ਚੰਨ ਨਾਲ ਹਰ ਰਾਤ ਚ,
ਚੜਦੇ ਹੀ ਸੂਰਜ ਉਹ ਹਾਵੀ ਹੋ ਜਾਂਦੀ ਆ ਮੇਰੇ ਦਿਲ ਦਿਮਾਗ ਚ,
ਜਿਸ ਕਮਲੀ ਦੀ ਤਸਵੀਰ ਸਾਂਭੀ ਮੈਂ ਆਪਣੀ ਕਿਤਾਬ ਚ।
ਦੀਪ ਸਤਿਕਾਰ

सफ़र...

सिर्फ शहर बदला है हम नहीं बदले
जो सीने में दफ़न हैं वो ग़म नहीं बदले

आज भी चलता हूँ मंजिल की और मैं
लड़खड़ाते रहे मगर कदम नहीं बदले

मेरे ख्याल में तेरा नज़रिया बदला है
तुम बदले मगर तुम्हारे सितम नहीं बदले

मुझसे मुहब्बत करती है कायनात सारी
अछा है कम से कम मौसम नहीं बदले।

दीप सतिकार

Karanpreet Singh Khanna

He is undergraduate student of agriculture department in Punjab agricultural University, ludhiana. He was born on 23 dec 2003 at khanna (punjab). A nature lover and simple person but significant by looks. He is a poet from inside to influence people with ideas .

ਫਰਕ ਨਹੀਂ ਪੈਂਦਾ

ਕੌਣ ਮੇਰੇ ਬਾਰੇ ਕੀ ਕਹਿੰਦਾ
ਮੈਨੂੰ ਫਰਕ ਰਤਾ ਨਹੀ ਪੈਦਾ,
ਜੋ ਤੇਰਾ ਮਿਹਣਾ ਦੇ ਕੇ ਛੱਡ ਰਹੇ
ਉਹਨਾ ਨਾਲ ਨਹੀ ਮੈ ਰਹਿੰਦਾ,

ਪਤਾ ਮੈਨੂੰ ਤੂੰ ਕਰ ਲੈਣਾ
ਜੋ ਵੀ ਤੂੰ ਸੋਚਦਾ ਰਹਿੰਦਾ ਏ,
ਨਾਲ ਖੜਾ ਹਰ ਪਲ ਤੇਰੇ
ਸੋਚੀ ਨਾ ਟੋਕਦਾ ਰਹਿੰਦਾ ਏ,

ਜੇਕਰ ਬੁਰਾ ਕਹਿੰਦੇ ਨੇ ਲੋਕ ਤੈਨੂੰ
ਤਾ ਬੁਰਾ ਬਣਨਾ ਏ ਮੰਜੂਰ ਮੈਨੂੰ,
ਕੋਈ ਪੁੱਠਾ ਪੈਡਾ ਫੜ ਲਏ ਨਾ
ਨਹੀ ਹੋਣ ਦਿੰਦਾ ਮਜਬੂਰ ਤੈਨੂੰ....

ਕਰਨਪ੍ਰੀਤ ਸਿੰਘ

ਬਿਆਨ-ਏ-ਕਲਮ

ਅਸੀਂ ਫੱਕਰ ਜਹੇ ਬੰਦੇ ਸੀ ਪਿੱਛੇ ਲੱਗ ਗਏ ਚੁਸਤ-ਚਲਾਕਾਂ ਦੇ, ਇੱਕ ਸੱਜਣ ਸਿੱਲ੍ਹ ਅੱਖਾ ਨੂੰ ਦੇ ਗਏ ਉਤੋਂ ਮੌਸਮ ਨੇ ਬਰਸਾਤਾਂ ਦੇ, ਉਹ ਬਾਜੀ ਵੀ ਹਾਰ ਕੇ ਬਹਿ ਗਏ ਜੋ ਖੇਡੀ ਨਾਲ ਜਜਬਾਤਾਂ ਦੇ, ਮੇਰੀ ਕਲਮ ਬਿਆਨ ਜੋ ਕਰ ਰਹੀ, ਸੱਜਣਾ ਦੀਆਂ ਸੁਗਾਤਾਂ ਨੇ, ਹਾਲੇ ਤਾ ਰੰਗ ਦਿਖਾਉਣੇ ਦੁਨੀਆਂ ਨੇ ਇਹ ਤਾ ਬੱਸ ਸੁਰੂਆਤਾ ਨੇ ਇਹ ਤਾ ਬੱਸ........

ਕਰਨਪ੍ਰੀਤ ਸਿੰਘ

ਟੁੱਟਿਆ ਦਿਲ

ਜੇ ਹੱਥ ਛੱਡਤਾ ਕੇਰਾ ਫਿਰ ਮੁੜਕੇ ਫੜ ਨਹੀ ਹੋਣਾ,

ਜੇ ਮੈ ਦਿਲ 'ਚੋਂ ਕੱਢਤਾ ਕੇਰਾ

ਫਿਰ ਮੁੜਕੇ ਦਿਲ ਵਿੱਚ ਵੜ ਨਹੀ ਹੋਣਾ, ਨਜਰਾਂ `ਚੋ ਡਿੱਗ ਪਈ ਇੱਕ ਵਾਰ ਜੇ ਫਿਰ ਮੁੜਕੇ ਉੱਠ

ਤੈਥੋ ਖੜ ਨਹੀ ਹੋਣਾ,

ਟੁੱਟਿਆ ਇੱਕ ਵਾਰ ਜੇ ਦਿਲ ਤਾ

ਇਲਜਾਮ ਕਿਸੇ ਸਿਰ ਮੜ ਨਹੀ ਹੋਣਾ,

ਗੱਲ ਮੁੱਕਦੀ ਇਹੋ ਆ ਸੱਜਣਾ ਜੇ ਮੈਂ ਹੁਣ ਚਲਾ ਗਿਆ ਤਾ ਫਿਰ ਵਾਪਿਸ ਮੁੜ ਨਹੀਂ ਆਉਣਾ.......

ਕਰਨਪ੍ਰੀਤ ਸਿੰਘ

ਕਿਤਾਬੀ ਰਾਸ

ਤੂੰ ਦਿਲ ਦੀ ਆ ਕਿਤਾਬ ਸੱਜਣਾਂ
ਕਦੇ ਦਿਲ ਦੇ ਵਰ ਕੇ ਫਰੋਲੇ ਨ੍ਹੀ...
ਆਪਣੀਆਂ ਲਿਖਤਾਂ ਦੇ. ਵਿੱਚ ਲਿਖੀ ਗਿਆ
ਪਰ ਪੜ੍ਹ ਹਕੇ ਕਦੇ ਬੋਲੇ ਨੀ...
ਬਣ ਕੇ ਰਹਿ ਗਿਆ ਰਾਜ ਸੱਜਣਾਂ
ਕਦੇ ਦਿਲ ਦੇ ਰਾਜ ਖੋਲੇ ਨੀ...
ਕਰਨਪ੍ਰੀਤ ਸਿੰਘ

ਦੁਨੀਆ

ਰੱਬ ਦੀ ਬਣਾਈ ਇਹ ਦੁਨੀਆਂ ਹਸੀਨ ਸੀ, ਕਰ ਦਿੱਤੀ ਏ ਤਬਾਅ ਜਿਹੜੀ ਜੰਨਤ ਜਮੀਨ ਸੀ,

ਕਰ ਕੇ ਕੋਸਿਸ਼ ਵੇਖੀ ਸਮਾਜ ਬਦਲਣ ਦੀ ,

ਪਰ ਜੱਗ ਦੀ ਨਿਗਾਹ 'ਚ ਇਹ ਜੁਰਮ ਸੰਗੀਨ ਸੀ,

ਦੇਖ ਕੇ ਹਲਾਤ ਚੱਲ ਰਹੇ ਦੌਰ ਦੇ ਅੱਖਾਂ 'ਚ ਸੀ ਸਿੱਲ,ਚਿੱਤ ਹੋਇਆ ਗਮਗੀਨ ਸੀ,

ਹੁਣ ਉਨੇ ਹੀ ਵਟਾਉਦੀ ਰੰਗ ਜਾਦੀ ਦੁਨੀਆਂ, ਪਹਿਲੀਆਂ 'ਚ ਜਿੰਨੀ ਇਹ ਦੁਨੀਆਂ ਰੰਗੀਨ ਸੀ.......

ਕਰਨਪ੍ਰੀਤ ਸਿੰਘ

ਅੰਤਰ

ਕੋਈ ਪੂਜਾ ਡਾਕੂਆਂ ਦੀ ਕਰਦਾ ਐ, ਕੋਈ ਪੜ੍ਹਦਾ ਇਸ਼ਕ ਦੇ ਲੇਖ ਸੱਜਣਾ। ਕੋਈ ਰੂਹਾਂ ਦਾ ਭੇਤੀ ਬੈਠਾ ਐ, ਤੇ ਕੋਈ ਹੁਸਨਾ ਨੂੰ ਰਿਹਾ ਦੇਖ ਸੱਜਣਾ, ਕੋਈ ਖੁੱਦ ਵਿਚ ਭਾਲੇ ਰੱਬ ਨੂੰ ਤੇ ਕੋਈ ਪਥਰ ਨੂੰ ਮੱਥੇ ਰਿਹਾ ਟੇਕ ਸੱਜਣਾ, ਕੋਈ ਜਿੰਦੜੀ ਤੋ ਡਰਦਾ ਨੇ ਤੇ ਕਈ ਸਮਝੀ ਬੈਠੇ ਇਹਨੂੰ ਖੇਡ ਸੱਜਣਾ।

ਕਰਨਪ੍ਰੀਤ ਸਿੰਘ

ਪਿੰਡ

ਚੱਲ ਮਿਤਰਾ ਮੁੜ ਪਿੰਡ ਨੂੰ ਚਲੀਏ
ਇਹ ਸ਼ਹਿਰ ਤਾਂ ਉਜੜੀ ਜਾਂਦੇ ਨੇ ...

ਸ਼ਹਿਰੀ ਘਰ ਨੇ ਬਣਗੇ ਜੇਲਾਂ ,
ਪਿੰਡ ਸੱਥੀਂ ਲੱਗਣ ਮੇਲੇ ,
ਮੁੜ-ਮੁੜ ਚੇਤੇ ਆਉਂਦੀਆਂ ਮਿਤਰਾ
ਗਲੀਆਂ ਜਿਥੇ ਖੇਲੇ ,
ਬਚਪਨ ਵਾਲੇ ਸੁਪਨੇ ਫਿਰ ਤੋਂ
ਦਿਲ ਵਿੱਚ ਉਮੜੀ ਜਾਂਦੇ ਨੇ ..
ਚੱਲ ਮਿਤਰਾ ਮੁੜ....

ਨਿੱਤ ਨਵਾਂ ਹੀ ਝਗੜਾ ਹੁੰਦਾ
ਮੰਦਿਰਾ ਤੇ ਮਸੀਤਾਂ ਦਾ ,
ਕੋਈ ਰਾਗ ਨਾ ਮਿਤਰਾ ਸੁਣਦਾ
ਜੱਟ ਯਮਲੇ ਦੇ ਗੀਤਾਂ ਦਾ ,
ਉਚਿਆਂ ਦੀਆਂ ਖੇਡਾਂ ਮਿਤਰਾ
ਸੱਭ ਪੈਸੇ ਨੂ ਚਿੰਬੜੀ ਜਾਂਦੇ ਨੇ ..
ਚੱਲ ਮਿਤਰਾ ਮੁੜ ਪਿੰਡ ਨੂੰ ਚਲੀਏ
ਇਹ ਸ਼ਹਿਰ ਤਾਂ ਉਜੜੀ ਜਾਂਦੇ ਨੇ ॥

ਵੱਡੇ-ਵੱਡੇ ਮਹਿਲ ਵੀ ਮੈਂ
ਖੰਡਰ ਹੁੰਦੇ ਵੇਖ ਲਏ ,
ਛੋਟੀ ਉਮਰੇ ਛੋਟਿਆਂ ਦੇ ਹੀ ਮੈਂ

ਕਿਨੇ ਹੀ ਸ਼ਿਵੇ ਸ਼ੋਕ ਲਏ ,

ਜ਼ੁਲਮ ਇਹ ਜ਼ਾਲਮ ਦੁਨਿਆ ਦੇ

ਮੈਨੂ ਝੰਝੋੜੀ ਜਾਂਦੇ ਨੇ ...

ਚੱਲ ਮਿਤਰਾ ਮੁੜ....

ਛੱਡ ਰਿਸ਼ਤੇ ਵਿੱਚ ਪਿੰਡਾਂ ਦੇ ਸ਼ਹਿਰੀ

ਬੁੱਤਾਂ ਵਰਗੇ ਹੋਗੇ ਨੇ ,

ਦੁਖ ਵਿੱਚ ਵੀ ਨਾ ਨਾਲ ਖੜਨ ਇਹ

ਰੁੱਤਾਂ ਵਰਗੇ ਹੋਗੇ ਨੇ ,

ਕਰਨ ਵਪਾਰ ਇਹ ਰਿਸਤਿਆਂ ਦਾ ਪੈਰੀਂ

ਲਾਸ਼ਾਂ ਲੁਤੜੀ ਜਾਂਦੇ ਨੇ ..

ਚੱਲ ਮਿਤਰਾ ਮੁੜ ਪਿੰਡ ਨੂੰ ਚਲੀਏ

ਇਹ ਸ਼ਹਿਰ ਤਾਂ ਉਜੜੀ ਜਾਂਦੇ ਨੇ।

ਕਰਨਪ੍ਰੀਤ ਸਿੰਘ

दीवाना

आप खूबसूरत हैं ही इतने कि हर शक्स की ज़ुबाँ पर आप ही का तराना है,
कोई शबद बाकी नहीं बचा आपकी तारीफ़ मे कुछ अलग ही अफसाना है,
बस एक ही ख्वाहिश बाकी है अगर मिलो कभी तो एक राज दिल का बताना है, हम नाचीज़ तो कहा किसी के काबिल
और आपका तो खुदा भी दीवाना हैं.....
करणप्रीत सिंह

एक तरफा

आपको क्या पता जनाब
कि एक तरफ से
प्यार का इज़हार करना क्या होता है,
जब नाराज़ हो कोई तो
उसे मनाने का अहसास क्या होता है,
जब जब भी वो कभी
दिल की एक भी बात करते है तब-तब हमारे दिल का क्या हाल होता है, उनकी मुस्कुराहट जान हैं हमारी आँसु एक भी
गहरी सोच मे डुबोता हैं,
जब सुनने मे आये कि खुशी के आँसु रोता है......
बहुत खुश हैं वो, तो यह दिल हमारा , खुशी के आंसु रोता है....

Navjot Singh

Navjot Singh is a poet who feels that the one thing he does best is writing poetry. He is a graduate of Punjab University and also has a degree in Hotel management. He has proven his talent for composing songs and singing in Punjabi music industry. He is a passionate person and is convinced that he would have gone insane if he had not been writing poetry. Writing is therapeutic for him. Therefore he considers pen and paper his true friends. He feels forever indebted to God for bestowing him with this talent.
Insta account : @jotnavee@Shehar_e_jazbaat

पगली

उसके और मेरे दर्मियां बस इतनी सी पहचान थी
कि,वो पगली मेरी ज़िंदगी में कुछ सालों की मेहमान थी
कभी झूम झूम के चलती थी
वो हर बात पे मस्ती करती थी
कभी गहरी सोच में खो जाती
तो कभी बोलते बोलते सो जाती
कभी 70 साल की बुढ़िया थी,कभी बच्चों सी शैतान थी
कि,वो पगली मेरी ज़िंदगी में......!
उसके होते दुख,दुख ना थे
ये होंठ मेरे यूं चुप ना थे
वो मेरा मैं उसका सहारा था
हर लम्हा मस्त आवारा था
ना उसके बगैर जीता था,मेरी बसती उसमें जान थी
कि,वो पगली मेरी ज़िंदगी में.......!
अब उम्र भर का रोना है
बस जागते जागते सोना है
कभी नई तो कभी पुरानी हैं
चीजें तो आनी जानी हैं
पर कैसे उसको भुलाऊं मैं,वो कौनसा कोई सामान थी
कि,वो पगली मेरी ज़िंदगी में.......!
हमें अपनों ने ही जुदा किया
बड़ी बेदर्दी से ज़िबाह किया
हम भी नासमझी कर बैठे
यूं ही आपस में लड़ बैठे
कुछ नवजोत ने वक्त संभाला ना,कुछ वो भी तो नादान थी
कि,वो पगली मेरी ज़िंदगी में.......!
बस इतनी सी पहचान थी.....!

धरती और आकाश

धरती और आकाश के जैसा रिश्ता है अपना,
इक दूजे को दिखते हैं पर मिल नहीं सकते...!
वाकिफ हैं कि,कभी भी मिलना न हो पाएगा,
फिर भी इक दूजे के सिवा कोई और नहीं तकते..!
हम गमले में पड़ी हुई मिट्टी के जैसे हैं,
हमने फूलों को खिलाया है,खुद खिल नहीं सकते...!
इश्क़ के कारोबार में तुम अभी कच्चे लगते हो,
हम रूह देने को राज़ी हैं,तुम दिल भी नहीं रखते...!
जैसे सूरज बिना रूके सदा रोशनी देता है,
हम प्यार बांटते रहते हैं,पर कभी नहीं थकते...!
जैसे भी हैं,औरों से हम बेहतर हैं 'नवजोत'
धर्मों की चादर ओढ़ के हम कभी ऐब है नहीं ढकते...!
नवजोत सिंह

ਮੈਂ ਹੀ ਮੇਰਾ ਹਾਂ

ਕੋਈ ਫਿਕਰ ਨਹੀਂ ਭਾਂਵੇ ਸਾਹਾਂ ਤੀਕ ਨੀਲਾਮ ਹੋਗੇ
ਅਸੀਂ ਰੱਜਕੇ ਆਪਣੀ ਲੁੱਟ ਦਾ ਜਸ਼ਨ ਮਨਾਉਂਦੇ ਆਂ
ਹੁਣ ਕੋਈ ਨੀ ਆਉਂਦਾ ਅੱਥਰੂ ਸਾਡੇ ਪੂੰਝਣ ਨੂੰ
ਅਸੀਂ ਆਪੇ ਰੋ ਕੇ ਆਪੇ ਈ ਚੁੱਪ ਕਰ ਜਾਨੇ ਆਂ
ਹੁਣ ਹਾਸਾ ਠਾਠਾ ਨਾਲ ਕਿਸੇ ਦੇ ਕਰਦੇ ਨਹੀਂ
ਬੱਸ ਕੱਲੇ ਈ ਹੱਸ ਹੱਸ ਆਪਣਾ ਖ਼ੂਨ ਵਧਾਉਂਦੇ ਆਂ
ਹੁਣ ਕੋਈ ਨੀ ਆਉਂਦਾ ....!
ਹੁਣ ਨਾਲ ਪਿਆਰ ਦੇ,ਨਾਮ ਲੈ ਕੋਈ ਬੁਲਾਉਂਦਾ ਨਹੀਂ
ਅਸੀਂ ਸ਼ੀਸ਼ੇ ਮੂਰੇ ਆਪਣਾ ਆਪ ਸਦਾਉਂਦੇ ਆਂ
ਹੁਣ ਕੋਈ ਨੀ ਆਉਂਦਾ ....!
ਰੌਲਿਆਂ ਰੱਪਿਆਂ ਦੇ ਵਿੱਚ ਬੜੀ ਗੁਜ਼ਾਰ ਲਈ
ਹੁਣ ਮੌਨ ਧਾਰ ਕੇ ਜ਼ਿੰਦਗੀ ਜਿਉਣਾ ਚਾਹੁੰਦੇ ਆਂ
ਹੁਣ ਕੋਈ ਨੀ ਆਉਂਦਾ ......!
ਅਸੀਂ ਆਦਤ ਤੋਂ ਮਜਬੂਰ ਬੜੇ 'ਨਵਜੋਤ' ਸਿਆਂ
ਪਹਿਲਾਂ ਪਿਆਰ ਵਧਾਕੇ ਪਿੱਛੋਂ ਫਿਰ ਪਛਤਾਉਂਦੇ ਆਂ
ਹੁਣ ਕੋਈ ਨੀ ਆਉਂਦਾ ਅੱਥਰੂ ਸਾਡੇ ਪੂੰਝਣ ਨੂੰ
ਅਸੀਂ ਆਪੇ ਰੋ ਕੇ ਆਪੇ ਈ .....!

ਨਵਜੋਤ ਸਿੰਘ

ਬਾਗ਼ੀ ਫ਼ਿਜ਼ਾ

ਕਦੋਂ ਹਵਾਵਾਂ ਕੀਤੀਆਂ ਨੇਂ ਕੈਦ ਕਿਸੇ ਨੇ,
ਕਦੋਂ ਰੰਗਾਂ ਦੀ ਰੰਗਤ ਨੂੰ ਕਿਸੇ ਲੁਕੋਇਆ ਏ
ਲੱਖ ਵਾਹ ਲਾਵੇ ਕੋਈ ਤੁਹਾਨੂੰ ਮਾਰ ਮੁਕਾਵਣ ਦੀ,
ਕਦੋਂ ਓਸ ਮਾਲਕ ਦੀ ਰਜ਼ਾ ਬਿਨਾਂ ਕੁਝ ਹੋਇਆ ਏ
ਕਦੋਂ ਕਿਸੇ ਦੇ ਆਖਿਆਂ ਕੋਈ ਚੁੱਪ ਹੈ ਕੀਤਾ,
ਤੇ ਕਦੋਂ ਕਿਸੇ ਦੇ ਆਖਿਆਂ ਕੁਝ ਹੋਇਆ ਏ
ਅਸਮਾਨ ਦੀ ਬੁੱਕਲ ਵਿੱਚ ਵੀ ਐਨੀਂ ਥਾਂ ਕਿੱਥੇ,
ਜਿੰਨਾ ਆਪਣੇ ਅੰਦਰ 'ਜੋਤ' ਨੇਂ ਦਰਦ ਸਮੋਇਆ ਏ
ਜੋ ਬੈਠਾ ਸਾਹਵੇਂ ਤੇਰੇ ਉਹ ਕੋਈ ਹੋਰ ਹੀ ਏ,
ਉਂਝ 'ਨਵਜੋਤ' ਤਾਂ ਯਾਰੋ ਕਦੋਂ ਦਾ ਮੋਇਆ ਏ
ਹੁਣ ਐਨੀਂ ਤਾਕ਼ਤ ਭਰ ਦਿੱਤੀ ਮੇਰੇ ਰੱਬ ਨੇਂ ਮੇਰੇ ਵਿੱਚ,
ਇੰਝ ਲੱਗਿਆ ਜਿਵੇਂ ਮੁਰਦਾ ਉੱਠ ਖਲੋਇਆ ਏ

ਨਵਜੋਤ ਸਿੰਘ

1*भीगना नहीं*

अच्छा लगता है खिड़की से बारिश को देखना,
मगर फिर से भीगने का हौंसला नहीं है

2*पहली या आखरी*

ख्वाब बनकर टूटने का दर्द तो बस वो ही जानें,
जिनकी पहली मुलाक़ात ही आखरी थी

3*बे बहर ज़िंदगी*

कुछ तो बहर में होजा ऐ जिंदगी मेरी,
कभी मैं भी तुझे गुनगुना के देख लूं

4*पक्की लकीर*

इस कदर दर्दों ने दामन पकड़ लिया है,
कि माथे की शिकन भी अब तो यारो पक सी गई है

5*पुनर विचार*

चल,इक दूजे को फिर से अजनबी बनकर मिलें,
क्या पता कि,हमें फिर से मुहब्बत हो जाए

6*क्या से क्या*

क्या बताऊं किस कदर टूटा हूं ज़िंदगी में,
बस यूं समझ लो,
कि एक खुला आसमां सिमट कर तिनका हो गया

7*खुलकर रोना है*

दावा है मेरा कि,आंखों से नदियां बहा दूंगा,
शर्त इतनी है कि,वो बैठी रहे मेरे सामने

8*औपचारिकता

साथ ए मोहब्बत उसका रेल की पटरी मानिंद था
कि मेरे संग रहकर भी उसने मुझसे फासला रखा

नवजोत सिंह

****

☟ SHERS ☟

****

1*गलती पे गलती*

जो चीज़ रूह को भा जाए,बस उसी में खो जाते हैं
हम एक ही गुस्ताख़ी बार बार करते हैं,
कि जिसके होते हैं,बस उसी के हो जाते हैं

2*कैसे जी गया?*

मैं कैसे जिऊंगा तेरे बिन,तेरे होते सोचता था,
आज तेरे बिना हूं जी रहा,पर सोचता नहीं

3*कठोर फूल*

जब आए दर्द चट्टानों से,तो रूह हस के मेरी सहार गई,
और जब चले इश्क के राहों पर,इक फूल की ठोकर मार गई

4*सीधी बात*

अजनबियों को भी गले लगाना,आदत है मेरी
मर मिटूं किसी के प्यार में,ये चाहत है मेरी
मेरी रूह को रोंदनें वालों में,आ तू भी ख़ुद को शामिल कर
आ मुझे आज़मा, इस्तेमाल कर और चलता बन

5*असल अमीरी बसती में*

कल,बसती में बच्चे टायर घुमाते खेलते हस्ते देखे
लाखों की मंहगी कारों को,मैंने तंज़ वो कसते देखे
हर मोड़ पे था जहां सबर शुक्र,मैंने ऐसे रस्ते देखे
वो सस्ते बहुत ही मंहगे थे और,मैंने मंहगे सस्ते देखे

6*वजह क्या है?*

मत पूछ क्यों तन्हा रहता हूं,तू रेहनें दे ख़ामोश मुझे
तुझे सब समझ आ जायेगा,तू मेरे ख्याल से सोच मुझे
तुनें हाथ थाम कर बोला था,कि सब ठीक हो जाएगा
कुछ भी तो ठीक नहीं हुआ,इसी बात का है अफसोस मुझे
मत पूछ क्यों तन्हा रहता हूं.....!
तू रेहनें दे....!

7*इस वक्त के कोठे पे मेरी हसरतें रोज बिकती हैं
हर रोज़ वक्त की ताल पे मेरी ज़िंदगी थिरकती है
मेरी हसरतों का मुजरा बड़ी दूर तक मशहूर है
मेरे दर्द को क्या जानेगी दुनिया नशे में चूर है

नवजोत सिंह

दिल का आशियाना

मेरी उम्मीदों के घराने पे हुआ हमला कातिलाना
जी भरके लूटा सबने मेरे दिल का आशियाना
कभी यार बनके लूटा, कभी प्यार बनके लूटा
कभी बनके दुश्मन सीने पे तलवार रखके लूटा
अपने ही थे जो लूट गए दिल अब तलक ना माना
जी भरके लूटा सबने......!
मेरी लूट ली जवानी,हुई ख्वाबों की नीलामी
छोड़ी नहीं दरिंदों ने इक पल की भी निशानी
कहां बैठूं अब सकून से,मेरा कोई नहीं ठिकाना
जी भरके लूटा सबने.....!
अपने ही घर में चोरों को देता रहा मैं दावत
बर्बाद कर गई यारो मुझको मेरी ये आदत
बड़ा सस्ते में नीलाम हुआ, उम्मीदों का खज़ाना
जी भरके लूटा सबने....!
रिश्तों का झूठा भरम था, इस दिल में मैंने पाला
इस दीवाने की अर्थी को कोई कंधा मत लगाना
अब नवजोत ने किसी से कोई रिश्ता नहीं निभाना
जी भरके लूटा सबने.....!
मेरे दिल का आशियाना.....!

तेरी एहमियत

शुक्र है जीते जी तुझसे मुलाक़ात तो हुई,
यादगार बन गया है अब मेरी ज़िंदगी का सफर
तुझको पाकर ज़िंदगी में,मैं कुछ तो पा सका
वरना नाकाम कहकर कोसता मैं खुदको उम्र भर
किस कदर हताश हूं मैं ज़िंदगी से यार,
तू समझ ही गया होगा मेरा हाल देखकर
चलो सिलसिला ए मुलाक़ात का आगाज़ तो हुआ,
अब देखते हैं कब तलक चलता है ये सफर
मैं अपने दीवानेपन को कैसे करू बयान
कुछ बोलने से पहले ही झुक जाती है नज़र
मैं कैसे बताऊं तुझको,क्या है आसरा तेरा
मिलती है हिम्मत मुझको,तेरा चेहरा देखकर
हद से बड़कर दिल ही दिल में चाहता हूं तुझको
लोगों की तरह टैटू बनवाकर करता नहीं नशर
मेरे शायराना तोहफे को,गर करले तू कबूल,
मैं समझूंगा मेरी शायरी में कुछ तो है असर
अब शौक से हो पाऊंगा मैं सपुर्द ए ख़ाक,
मिल लिया हूं अपने प्यार से,अब कोई नहीं फिकर
इस ज़िंदगी से नवजोत को बस है यही शिकवा,
क्यों उड़ ना सके ख़्वाब मेरे पंख लगाकर

रज़ा या सज़ा

है उसकी रज़ा में मज़ा ही मज़ा
ना मानो रज़ा,तो सज़ा ही सज़ा
हस्ता रहा कर हसाता रहा कर
रूठे लोगों को मनाता रहा कर
मनाता है वो ही सताता भी वो ही
उजाड़े भी वो ही बसाता है वो ही
है उसकी रज़ा में .....! ना मानो रज़ा तो....!
ये पानी वही है,समंदर वो ही है
समंदर में उठता भवंडर वो ही है
ये मेले भी उसके,ये खंडर वो ही है
बाहर भी वो है,तेरे अंदर वो ही है
है उसकी रज़ा में .....! ना मानो रज़ा तो....!
गर,मानो तो सब कुछ वो ही है करता
ना मानो तो,सब कुछ हमनें किया है
चलो मान लो,कि सब हमनें किया है
पर करने को,दिमाग किसने दिया है
है उसकी रज़ा में .....! ना मानो रज़ा तो....!
तू खोजे जहां पे वहां वो नहीं है
ढूंढे तू उसको,खोया जो नहीं है
मिलाना,मिलाकर जुदा करता वो ही
बंदे से तुझको खुदा करता वो ही
है उसकी रज़ा में .....! ना मानो रज़ा तो....!
वो करता है वो ही,जो भाता है उसको
वो मिलता उसे,जो निभाता है उसको
खुले आम फिरता पर दिखता नहीं है
छिप कर भी दुनियां से छिपता नहीं है
है उसकी रज़ा में .....! ना मानो रज़ा तो....!
हंसता वही है और रोता भी वो ही
सितारों के सपने संजोता भी वो ही
पाता वही है और खोता भी वो ही
जो भाता है उसको,है होता भी वो ही
है उसकी रज़ा में .....! ना मानो रज़ा तो....!
यहां जो भी होता वो,वो ही है करता

तू काहे को नवजोत फिकरों में मरता
इस सूरज से परदा वो ही तो उठाए
इन तारों में ज्योति,वो ही तो जगाए
है उसकी रज़ा में,
मज़ा ही मज़ा....!
ना मानो रज़ा तो,
सज़ा ही सज़ा....!
नवजोत सिंह

Gurjeet Kumar

॥ਹੌਲ਼ੀ ਹੌਲ਼ੀ ਸੁਧਾਰ ਰਹੇ ਹਾਂ ਲਿਖਾਵਟ,

ਮੈਨੂੰ ਸੋਂਹਦੀ ਬਹੁਤੀ ੳ ਤੋਂ ਲ਼ ਦੀ ਬਣਾਵਟ ॥

ਗੁਰਜੀਤ ਫਰੀਦਕੋਟ ਜਿਲ੍ਹੇ ਦੇ ਨਿੱਕੇ ਜੇ ਪਿੰਡ ਬਾਹਮਣਵਾਲਾ ਦਾ ਵਸਨੀਕ ਹੈ। ਪੰਜਾਬ ਐਗਰੀਕਲਚਰਲ ਯੂਨੀਵਰਸਿਟੀ, ਲੁਧਿਆਣਾ ਤੋਂ ਬੈਚਲਰ ਦੀ ਪੜ੍ਹਾਈ ਪੂਰੀ ਕਰਕੇ ਹੁਣ ਕੈਨੇਡਾ ਦੇ ਲੰਬਟਨ ਕਾਲਜ ਵਿੱਚ ਮਾਸਟਰਜ਼ ਕਰ ਰਿਹਾ ਹੈ।

ਕਵਿਤਾ ਅਤੇ ਨਾਟਕ ਪ੍ਰੇਮੀ

gurjeetsharma9990@gmail.com
+14379806521

ਪੌਣੇ ਕੋਹ ਦੀ ਵਾਟ*

*ਰੁਕਸਤ ਕਰਨਾ ਤੇ ਰੁਕਸਤ ਹੋਣਾ,
ਬੰਦਾ ਕੀ ਐ,ਰੱਬ ਦੇ ਹੱਥ ਖਿਡੌਣਾ,
ਕਾਹਲ 'ਚ ਸਿਉਤਾ ਆਖਰੀ ਕੱਪੜਾ,
ਦੱਸ ਕਿੱਥੇ ਗਿਆ ਤਦ ਫੈਸ਼ਨ ਤੇਰਾ,

ਪੌਣੇ ਕੋਹ ਤੇ ਪਿੰਡੋਂ ਮੜ੍ਹੀਆਂ ਅੜਿਆਂ,

ਸੱਚ ਜਾਣੀ ਰਾਹ ਬੜਾ ਲੰਮੇਰਾ।
*ਖ਼ਲਕਤ ਘੁੰਮੀ ਸੁਣਿਆ ਤੈਅ ਹੋਸਾ ਹੋ ਕੇ,
ਆਪਣਿਆਂ ਤੋਰ ਦਿੱਤਾ ਤੈਨੂੰ ਹਫਤਾ ਕੁ ਰੋ ਕੇ,
ਕੁਝ ਵਹਾਏ ਹੰਝੂ ਘਰ ਦੀ ਹਦੂਦ ਅੰਦਰ,
ਕੁਝ ਵਿਦਾ ਕਿਤਾ ਕਰ ਤੱਕੜਾ ਜੇਰਾ,
ਪੌਣੇ ਕੋਹ ਤੇ ਪਿੰਡੋਂ ਮੜ੍ਹੀਆਂ ਅੜਿਆਂ,
ਸੱਚ ਜਾਣੀ ਰਾਹ ਬੜਾ ਲੰਮੇਰਾ।

*ਪੈਰ ਜ਼ਮੀਨ ਤੇ ਲੱਗਣੇ ਨਹੀਂ,
ਹੁਣ ਕੂਚ ਜਮਾ ਕੇ ਕਰਦਾ ਏ,
ਉਹ ਤੇਰੇ ਅੰਦਰ ਤੋਂ ਵੀ ਜਾਣੂ,
ਤੂੰ ਗੁਨਾਹ ਰੱਬ ਤੋਂ ਲੁੱਕਾ ਕੇ ਕਰਦਾ ਏ,
ਸਿਵਿਆਂ 'ਚ ਅੱਗ ਤੋਂ ਰਾਖ ਹੋਇਆ,
ਪਈਆਂ ਤਰਕਾਲਾਂ ਹੋਇਆਂ 'ਨ੍ਹੇਰਾ,
ਪੌਣੇ ਕੋਹ ਤੇ ਪਿੰਡੋਂ ਮੜ੍ਹੀਆਂ ਅੜਿਆਂ,
ਸੱਚ ਜਾਣੀ ਰਾਹ ਬੜਾ ਲੰਮੇਰਾ।

*ਭਾਣਾ ਰੱਬ ਦਾ ਮੰਨ ਬੰਦੇ,
ਬਣ ਕਿਸੇ ਦੇ ਦੁੱਖ ਦੀ ਦਵਾ ਦਾਰੂ,
ਸਿੱਕਿਆਂ ਤੋਂ ਕੁਝ ਖੱਟ ਨੀ ਹੁੰਦਾ,
ਅਮਰ ਹੋ ਜਾਂਦੇ ਨੇ ਜੁਝਾਰੂ,
ਹਜੇ ਵੀ ਸਮਝ ਲੈ ਤਰਕ ਬੰਦੇ,
ਕੁਝ ਵਿਗੜਿਆਂ ਨੀ ਡੁੱਲ੍ਹੇ ਬੇਰਾਂ,
ਪੌਣੇ ਕੋਹ ਤੇ ਪਿੰਡੋਂ ਮੜ੍ਹੀਆਂ ਅੜਿਆਂ,
ਸੱਚ ਜਾਣੀ ਰਾਹ ਬੜਾ ਲੰਮੇਰਾ |

ਆਦਤ ਜਾਂ ਪਿਆਰ

ਹੰਢਾਲੇ ਚੀਰੇ ਰੂਹ ਤੇ,

ਕਿੰਨੀ ਤਿੱਖੀ ਖੰਜਰ ਦੀ ਧਾਰ
ਅਸੀਂ ਸਮਝ ਨਹੀਂ ਪਾਏ,

ਹੱਸ ਕੇ ਬੋਝ ਚੁੱਕ ਲਿਆ,
ਕਿੰਨਾ ਦੁੱਖਾਂ ਦਾ ਭਾਰ
ਅਸੀਂ ਸਮਝ ਨਹੀਂ ਪਾਏ,

ਵਿੱਚ ਵਾਅ ਵਰੋਲੇ ਦਿਖਿਆਂ ਕੁਝ ਨਾ,
ਕਿੱਥੇ ਗਵਾਚੀਆਂ ਅੱਖਾਂ ਚਾਰ
ਅਸੀਂ ਸਮਝ ਨਹੀਂ ਪਾਏ,

ਬੋਲਣਾ ਉਹਦਾ ਪਸੰਦ ਸੀ ਸਾਨੂੰ ,

ਇਹ ਆਦਤ ਸੀ ਜਾਂ ਪਿਆਰ

ਅਸੀਂ ਸਮਝ ਨਹੀਂ ਪਾਏ

ਚੀਜ਼ ਦੀ ਤਵੱਜੋ

ਛਿਪਣ ਵਾਲੇ ਸੂਰਜ ਨੂੰ ਪੁੱਛੀ ਹਨੇਰੇ ਦਾ ਖੌਫ
ਤੇ ਚੜ੍ਹਣ ਵਾਲੇ ਚੰਨ ਨੂੰ ਸੂਰਜ ਦਾ ਮੇਲ ਪੁੱਛੀ,

ਮੁੱਕੀ ਸਿਆਹੀ ਦੇ ਲਫਜਾਂ ਨੂੰ ਕਾਗਜ਼ ਦੀ ਕਦਰ
ਤੇ ਪੰਜਾਬੀ ਦੀ ਪਈ ਸੁੱਕਦੀ ਕਿਉਂ ਂ ਵੇਲ ਪੁੱਛੀ,

ਬੰਦੀ ਪੰਛੀ ਤੋਂ ਸੁਪਨਾ ਹਵਾਈ ਉੱਡਣੇ ਦਾ,
ਤੇ ਲਾਲਚੀ ਨੇਤਾ ਨੂੰ ਨਾ ਹੋਣ ਵਾਲੀ ਜੇਲ੍ਹ ਪੁੱਛੀ,

ਪਰ ਕਦੇ,
ਪ੍ਰਭਾਵਤ ਹੋਏ ਲਿਖਾਰੀ ਨੂੰ ਨਾ ਪੁੱਛੀ ਵੱਲ ਲਿਖਣੇ ਦਾ,
ਤੇਰੇ ਖਿਆਲ ਦੀ ਦੁਨੀਆਂ ਨੂੰ ਰੂਹੀ ਖੇਲ ਪੁੱਛੀ

ਕੁਝ ਵੱਖਰਾ

ਮੱਚ ਬੁੱਝੀ ਸੀਖ ਦੇ ਸੰਤਾਪ ਬਾਰੇ,
ਜਾਂ ਡੱਬੀ ਦੇ ਬਾਰੂਦ ਦੀ ਔਕਾਤ ਲਿਖੇਗਾ,

ਟਿਮ ਟਿਮਾਉਂਦੇ ਲਾਟੂਆਂ ਦੀ ਦਿਵਾਲੀ,
ਜਾਂ ਕਿਸਾਨ ਦੀ ਕਾਲੀ ਰਾਤ ਲਿਖੇਗਾ,

ਸਰਿੰਜਾਂ 'ਚ ਕੈਦ ਪੰਜਾਬ ਦੀ ਜਵਾਨੀ,
ਚਾਹੁੰਦੀ ਜਾਣਨਾ ਤੂੰ ਕਿਹਦੀ ਬਾਤ ਲਿਖੇਗਾ,

ਕਲਮ ਨੂੰ ਭਰਾ ਨਿਖਾਰੀ ਸੋਚ ਦਾ ਹੁੰਗਾਰਾ,
ਕਦ ਤੱਕ ਟੁੱਟੇ ਦਿਲਾਂ ਦੇ ਦੁਖਾਂਤ ਲਿਖੇਗਾ

ਖੁਸ਼ੀ

ਡੁੱਬਦੇ ਸੂਰਜ ਤੋਂ ਮੰਗੀ ਲਾਲੀ ਮੁੱਖੜੇ ਲਈ,
ਤੇ ਚੜ੍ਹਦੇ ਤੋਂ ਹਾਸੇ ਤੂੰ ਉਧਾਰ ਲਈ,

ਕਲਾ ਨੂੰ ਬੰਨ੍ਹ ਨਾ ਫਿਕਰਾਂ ਦੇ ਰੱਸੇ,
ਬੇਫਿਕਰਾ ਹੋ ਕੇ ਹੁਨਰ ਖਿਲਾਰ ਲਈ,

ਲੱਖਾਂ ਲੁੱਟਾਏ ਜੋ ਨਹੀਂ ਲੱਧਿਆ,
ਬੱਚੇ ਨੂੰ ਬਸਤਾ ਦੇ ਬੋਝ ਉਤਾਰ ਲਈ,

ਪੈਸਾ ਚੁਰਾਏ ਤਾਂ ਤਮ੍ਹਾ ਨਹੀਂ ਭਰਨੀ,
ਮੇਰੀ ਮੰਨੇ ਕਿਤਾਬੋਂ ਲੁੱਟ ਵਿਚਾਰ ਲਈ

Ashna Kaur

An educator by profession, firmly believe in God. She also feel that words possess the divine power to touch the lives of others.

Mailid: ashnamht@gmail.com

Radiance of Life

Life is best lived when
You devote every ounce
Of your being in creating
A world where the value
To peace is given utmost
Importance, where people
With all their might strive
Their hardest and bring
Glory, in each and everything
They do. The world where
The meaning of humanity
Is understood in its correct
Essence, The world where
There is no fear in the hearts
And minds of anyone. The
World where everyone lives with
A sense of security and are totally
At ease, the world where people
Don't abandon hope and strength
To live is something which makes

Life more beautiful.

The values making our belief
System more strong, inspiring us to
Achieve great heights and enabling us
To never give up. The world where
Love and harmony pervading in
Nook and corner transcending
All the barriers, uniting everyone
Making our foundation rock solid.
The world where so much emphasis
Is on bringing out the best in all
Where there is no discrimination
With people, freely and fully
Exhibiting and radiating positivity.
For in such a type of world we
Can all the more reckon our life force
And not only achieve what we desire
But what we truly deserve.

-Ashna Kaur

Quotes

With a strong inner resolve.. You can conquer the world..

-Ashna Kaur

The sun is a teacher, whose brilliance and warmth infuses a vibrant spirit in us.

-Ashna Kaur

Faith in three words means to

"Never Give Up".

-Ashna Kaur

THE END

For contacting publication, VISIT:

Website:- www.sotpublication.com

Instagram:- https://www.instagram.com/spectrum.of.thoughts/

Linkedin:- https://www.linkedin.com/company/spectrum-of-thoughts

Twitter:- https://twitter.com/spectrumpublish

www.ingramcontent.com/pod-product-compliance
Lightning Source LLC
Chambersburg PA
CBHW031351230926
51848CB00002B/473
9789354525124